I HEARD YOU WERE DEAD

JOSEPH GIULIANI

This book is a work of fiction. Names, characters, businesses, places, events and incidents are either products of the author's imagination or used in a fictitious manner. Any resemblance to actual persons, living or dead, or actual events is purely coincidental.

CHAPTER 1

The petite brunette with the gorgeous figure strolled into my office on one spectacular Monday morning in May. She carried in the freshness of a new spring day and the fragrance of daffodils. She sat in the chair in front of my desk, crossed one slender leg over the other, and introduced herself.

"My name is Phyllis Steele," she said. "Are you Mr. Caruso? Joe Caruso, the private detective?"

Mooching an overused cliché, I said. "Miss. Steele, I can be anyone you wish."

"It's Mrs. Steele," she said. "And I'm happily married so you can close that gap in your face, Mr. Caruso."

"Pardon my gawking. It isn't every day that a beautiful woman walks into my office."

She looked around the office with a skeptical eye.

"By the look of your office, I wonder if you receive anyone at all," she said.

"Touché. What can I do for you, Mrs. Steele?"

"Phil. My friends call me Phil."

"Okay, Phil, it is. So Phil, who do you want me to bump off?"

She gasped. "How did you know?"

"I was joking."

"Of course," she said.

She appeared unhappy about that. I'm really not in the business of killing anyone. At least not just anyone. I have made exceptions to that rule, but now wasn't the time or place to tell her that.

She unclasped her pocketbook and removed a standard size photograph. Cautiously, as if the man in the photo would spring to life and bite her finger, she slid the picture across the desk. The mug shot was of a hatchet-faced man with a snub nose, tight lips, and hostile eyes.

"I want you to find him," she said.

"Who is he?" I asked.

"His name is Julio Silva," she answered. "He can be dangerous," she said, brushing a strand of ink-black hair away from soft grey eyes that hinted that she was frightened of the man.

"Has he threatened you?" I asked.

Her expression turned as stone-faced as the Mona Lisa and as cold as a Siberian kiss. "I want him found, and that's all you need to know."

"I'll need to know more."

She leaned over and placed her arms on the desk. "Joe. I can call you, Joe, can't I?" She batted long eyelashes over those charming soft grey eyes.

"I've been called worse, so Joe will do just fine," I said.

Long lashes and soft grey eyes turn me into putty every time.

She reached inside that purse again, but this time her hand came out clutching a crisp new $100-dollar bill. She slid the cash across the desk to me.

"There is more where this comes from, Joe."

"How much more?" I asked.

"Do you always ask so many questions."

"Asking questions helps to keep me out of trouble."

"Do you think that I'm trouble, Joe?"

"We just met. For all, I know you could be a saint."

She giggled. "I'm no saint, Joe."

"I'll be on the up and up with you, Mrs. Steele. I have, on occasion, turned down an attractive lady."

"Phil," she said. She pushed the money closer.

"Phil," I said. I snatched up the bill. "But I have never turned away Benjamin Franklin. I'll take your case."

Her hand went back to her purse. I waited for the hat trick. Maybe this time a rabbit or white dove would appear from the purse. It was a business card. She handed it to me. It isn't often that a woman gives me a business card, especially since this woman didn't have a business per se to advertise. I turned the card over in my hand. The paper felt like silk. The color, crystal white with burgundy English script that spelled out the name Brooks Herrington. His telephone number and address in muted print just below his signature.

"I don't want my husband to know about our arrangement, Joe. Call Brooks whenever you need to contact me. He'll know how to get hold of me."

"Who is he?" I asked.

"Brooks is a friend," she answered.

"A boyfriend?"

"No, just a friend."

I examined the card once more while rolling his name over my tongue. It didn't taste right.

"No, he isn't a friend," I said. "The name doesn't fit a friend's name. It sounds more like a shrink's name. A head doctor. A psychiatrist. Is he your psychiatrist?" I asked.

She wiggled uncomfortably in her chair before straightening her back and locking her eyes on mine. "Yes," she replied. "I have an impulsive desire to fall in love with every man I meet. Doctor Herrington is treating me."

"Now, things are looking up," I said.

She darted to her feet. "Unfortunately for you, Mr. Caruso, I never mix business with pleasure."

She walked out, and I watched every move as she left through the door. I thought about handling her case Pro Bono considering the benefits. But, phooey, I needed the money.

Phyllis Steele left me holding a $100 bill, a picture of a man that could be anywhere in a big city like Chicago, and my heart in my hand. I shoved the photo and the money in a pocket, put on my hat, and took my revolver out of the desk drawer. Something told me that homicide was a good place to begin looking for Julio Silva.

CHAPTER 2

With spring in the air, the late morning sun felt warm, and the air smelled fresh. The tall buildings propped up a sky of perfect robin's egg blue. Peaks of whipped cream colored clouds hung randomly in the sky. The pleasant morning gave me a pretty good feeling. That feeling turned sour when my taxi stopped in front of the 52nd prescient. The exterior finished in a depressing brown enamel brought me down. The thought of facing Lieutenant Shakespeare, the first thing in the morning, or for that matter, at any time of the day was never a pleasant task. I almost didn't want to get out of the taxi. Telling the driver to take me to Grant Park or Brookfield Zoo would be easy. But I didn't. I paid the driver and got out of his cab. I took the three concrete steps that lead to the double door entrance. A sheet of plywood replaced the glass on one of the doors. Two uniform cops stood outside the doors, smoking cigarettes and talking. They stopped talking as I passed to go inside.

Two disorderly ladies shouted obscenities at the two cops who dragged them off the street and into the prescient. One lady had red hair the color of a sunset. The other a blond. A blond wig tilted on her head exposed dark roots. I wondered what else was false about her. They both wore mini skirts. The blonde's skirt being shorter than her friend's. A drunk sat in a corner. He was dressed in a woolen sport coat, a White Sox tee shirt with a faded logo, kaki pants and brown sneakers. He sang Happy Birthday over and over at the top of his lungs. I tipped my hat to the desk sergeant and took the stairs two at a time to the homicide department on the second floor.

I HEARD YOU WERE DEAD

When I think about the five years I worked homicide it comes to me as a blur. Most of those days I spent higher than a kite. I came to work buzzed so I couldn't feel the depression. These days I'm of a leveler head. I notice things. I see how the globe light fixtures hanging from the ceiling never give off enough light. Forget about any sunlight coming through the windows. The glass is so caked yellow with nicotine stains a spotlight couldn't crash that dirt. Metal desk drawers squeak when pulled open, and they clank hard when pushed closed. The telephone and the people are annoying. The people yell, swear, and some even cry. The phone never stops ringing.

Cops come and go. A few retire and some transferred to other departments. Unfortunately, one or two die in the line of duty. I don't recognize these detectives. Another detective is sitting at my old desk. He's welcome to it.

Shakespeare was in shirt sleeves, sitting at his desk, his light brown suit jacket casually draped over the chair back. He was leaning as far back as his chair would allow. His fedora tilted on his head blocked the glare from the office lights. His eyes were closed and relaxed, but he held his cigar tight between his lips. His hands were folded on top of his ample gut.

I knocked on the door frame and stepped inside.

"You, here again, Caruso?" Shakespeare said, without so much as opening his eyes.

"Did you miss me?" I said.

"I miss you, Caruso like I miss a case of diarrhea. What do you want? And make it snappy. I've been here all night and probably will be here all day."

"I'm looking for a man," I said.

"Try the county morgue. I hear they have a fresh group of stiffs."

He straightened. The chair creaking as it resumed its natural upright position. Shakespeare angled his cigar in an ashtray first flicking the ash off.

I handed Shakespeare the picture of Silva. He gave the picture as much attention as he would a discarded gun wrapper.

"His name is Julio Silva, and he's dangerous," I said adding that last bit of flourish to make a point.

"I know who Silva is," Shakespeare said.

He flipped the photo back to me. It did a summersault in mid-air, bounced off the corner of the desk and fell to the floor. I leaned over and picked it up.

"He's an ex-boxed," Shakespeare said. "He did some fighting in a bar when he should have been fighting in the ring. He's doing time in State. As long as he stays locked up, he's not dangerous. But put him on the street and he's as crazy as a deranged ape. Why are you interested in Silva?"

"My client wants him found," I said.

"Tell your client Silva's address is the Illinois State Petitionary. Visiting hours are eleven to two o'clock Monday, Wednesday, and Friday."

"The way she talks Silva might be out," I said.

Shakespeare shrugged and pulled back a yawn. "That's not my thing. Check with the parole board." He yawned again. "Why do you keep coming back?" he asked.

"Bad habits are hard to break," I said.

"Let me help you. There's the door. Leave by it."

CHAPTER 3

The Daily News Building sits on the east bank of the Chicago River. On humid summer days, the smell of the algae from the river mixes with the scent of printing ink from the presses. The combined smells are sickening. Yet hundreds of people work inside the building without experiencing ill effects. Katrina Warring is one of those loyal reporters.

I rode the elevator up to the fifth floor. The newsroom is where reporters craft their columns and articles. Where front-page stories originate, editorials get dressed up; social columnists scoop the variety scene for gossip and where crimes get reported. Katrina is the chief crime reporter for the newspaper. The fifth floor usually is active, but today it went crazy. The ringing of telephones and the clanking of typewriter keys never fell silent for a second. The copyboys, famed for yelling obscenities from desk to desk, shouted louder. The newsroom was in chaos.

I landed at Katrina's desk. The uneasy look on her face could only mean one thing. Something serious had happened.

"Rough morning?" I said.

Katrina looked up. "Late last night, a prominent attorney and former judge was found dead."

"People die," I said.

"This one took a short cut out of his sixth-floor bedroom window."

"Jumped?"

"Thrown," she said. "Right through the plate glass."

"Ouch. Who is the lawyer?"

"Frederick Ore," she said. "You don't remember him?"

I shrugged. "No. Should I?"

"Judge Ore presided over the Domenic Conte murder. Remember now? You arrested and testified against the tart who killed Conte in his hotel room," she said.

"That tart's name is Maria Savona," I said.

"A name is a name, and a tart is a tart," she said.

"No wonder Shakespeare was asleep in his office," I said.

"You saw Lieutenant Shakespeare this morning?"

"Unfortunately, yes. He didn't say anything about murder if that's what you're thinking. I'm chasing a missing person, and I thought a good starting point was homicide. My client is Phyllis Steele. Have you heard of her?"

"I sure do know a thing or two about Phyllis Steele," Katrina said. "She's married to Edward Steele. He has deep pockets, and she has her hands in them. Mrs. Steele is colorful. You want their biographies, or will the table of contents do?"

"I'll take the short version," I said.

Katrina picked up a pencil and made a doodle on a pad of paper.

"Edward Steele is fifty-nine years old and is sinfully rich," she said. "He owns a chain of hardware stores in three states; Illinois, Wisconsin, and Indiana."

"There is that much money in selling nuts and screws?" I asked.

Katrina nodded. "Steele may be connected to an unsavory crowd. That would suggest how he gets his money. But that rumor never was substantiated. What is surprising is that Jerry Pascoe was Steele's long-time friend and partner in several business ventures."

"That's substantiated evidence enough for me," I said. "Jerry Pascoe was a fly by night gangster who had his fingers in more pies than a baker. Tell me about Phyllis Steele."

"Three words: beautiful, glamorous, and bloodsucker. Phyllis goes by the nickname Phil," Katrina said. "She danced in Vegas and Hollywood before settling in Chicago and marrying Steele. Nowadays, she occupies her time, spending her husband's money. Jewelry and clothing are one and two on her buying list. Young men are third."

"What about a man named Brooks Herrington?" I asked.

"No, never heard of him," Katrina said. "Sounds like a movie star's name."

"He's a shrink."

"I still haven't heard of him. So, who is this missing person you saw Shakespeare about?"

I handed Katrina the photo of the man Phyllis Steele paid me to locate.

"Do you know who this is?" she asked.

"His name is Julio Silva," I said.

"Julio Silva was a heavyweight boxer who beat a man to near death in a barroom brawl. Judge Ore sentenced Silva to five years in prison for that crime."

"And once again, Judge Fredrick Ore's name pops up," I said.

"The same judge who sentenced Maria Savona," she said.

"Silva was Julio's professional name. Savona is his real name. He's Maria Savona's brother."

"Maria Savona, the girl who killed Domenic Conte?"

Katrina nodded. "The girl you put in jail for life."

CHAPTER 4

My neighbor is a former lightweight boxer. Sportswriters tagged Duck Rizzo, with the nickname Duck because Rizzo never ducked a punch. He caught so many blows to the head doctors warned him about fighting again. One more head punch and he would be down for the count. So Duck retired and bought the convenience store next to my building.

Duck wasn't inside his store, so I walked around back and climbed the stairs to his flat. I knocked on the door. Duck answered, wearing shorts and a tee top.

"I just got home from the gym," he said, letting me inside his apartment. "I'm working out doing a bit of shadow boxing, punching the heavy bag, that sort of thing."

"You're not doing any sparing, are you?" I asked. "You know what the doctor said."

"No sir, Joe. My days of getting hit are over. You want coffee I just brewed a pot."

We sat at Duck's kitchen table and drank coffee. Duck drank his coffee, Irish. With a splash of Jameson Whiskey. I kept mine black.

"You ever hear of a heavyweight named Julio Silva?" I asked.

"Sure," Duck said, blowing steam off the lip of the coffee cup. "Silva was a good prospect until he got his clock cleaned by some Polack fighter. A big mutt. Bohater, or Kowo something. Word had it that Silva's managers had him throw that fight. They took the long end cash on the Polack and Silva got the short end. Anyway, I heard Silva got himself into trouble. Did time in the pokey."

"Silva got five years for attempted manslaughter," I said.

Duck poured more coffee. This time I took mine with a shot of whiskey.

"Tough break," Duck said. "Boxing is a brutal business inside and outside of the ring. The promoters try to pull boxing off as a sport. They call it the sweet science, hoping no one notices the blood. Boxing is nothing more than gladiators fighting in a coliseum. Hell, if they could put lions in the ring with the fighters, they would."

I declined a refill on the coffee for straight whiskey.

"Where do ex-fighters hangout?" I asked.

"You mean at a gym?"

"Sure. You pugs have sawdust in your veins. After what you've been through, you still hit the bag once in a while."

Duck flinched — an automatic reaction. "Try the A-Street Boxing Gym on Madison. That's where I work out. Or the

YMCA on Polk Street. Hey, Joe, why is this Silva on your radar? Isn't one ex-pug in your life enough?"

I grabbed the bottle and refreshed my drink.

"You're a friend, Duck. My gut feeling tells me that this ex-pug isn't friendly."

CHAPTER 5

I got out of Duck's apartment just before he poured more Jameson into my cup. A fuzzy booze drenched head I didn't need. I caught up to a taxi unloading a couple at curbside and nudged my way inside. Evening had taken the place of afternoon. The night was warm but hazy with fog rolling off Lake Michigan. I rolled down the window of the taxi, hung my elbow out, and watched the smoke from my cigarette somersault into the night. A light wind blowing from the east to west carried the scent of fried smelt from the shore of the lake. In Chicago, the running of the smelt, those slender sliver fish that shore fishermen catch, bread and fry right from the water and then eat head, bones and all, signaled our early

spring. I sat back and enjoyed the drive.

The taxi cruised to a stop in front of the YMCA. I told the

driver to wait and got out. This building, like all of the other

buildings along Printer's Row, saw considerable overhaul a

few years back. One look around the gym, and I knew that a

mug the likes of Julio Silva wouldn't be caught dead in a place

like this. But since I was there, I decided to ask around. No

one heard of Julio Silva.   Silva needed an old school blood

and guts fighting gym to feel comfortable. I got back into the

taxi and gave the drive the address to the A-Street Boxing

Club.

An old black gentleman sitting on a high stool at the door

stopped me from going inside. A dirty Panama hat sat tilted on

his head. A section of the brim torn off. He looked up at me from over a copy of Ring Magazine. The scars on his face read like a McNally road map of brutal fights.

"Five bucks if you want to work out," he said. "Punch the bags is an extra buck. Locker is fifty cents. Towels a quarter."

"I'm looking for a fighter," I said.

"You a cop? The boys don't like cops. If you're a cop, you had better beat it."

"I'm not a cop," I said.

"And you ain't no fighter either cuz by the look of your face you been on the losing side of a struggle one too many times. Maybe you should sign up for boxing lessons."

"I'm looking for an ex-heavyweight. Julio Silva."

"Never heard of him," the old man said.

"What's going on here?" a voice said.

The voice spoke broken English with a thick Polish accent.

The man that belonged to the voice wasn't lean, fast, and stealth-like a boxer. He was thick with fat over muscle like an out of shape weightlifter. His face was squared and chiseled. Very European looking. A toothpick clenched between his lips, no doubt a substitute for a cigar or cigarette. The pale color of his face contradicted the flashy color of the red-flowered Hawaiian shirt he wore untucked under a beige sports coat. His attire looked as out of fashion in Chicago as a parka would in Florida.

"This fella wants in," the old man said. "He's asking about a fighter — a heavyweight. I told him to scram. He smells like bacon to me."

"You a cop?" the broken English voice asked.

"No, I'm not a cop," I said. "I'm a private investigator, and I'm looking for an ex-heavyweight fighter who goes by the name Julio Silva.

"I'm Alex Popovich," he said. "I run this gym. You are?"

"Joe Caruso," I said.

"In my country, Joe Caruso, there is no difference between a private detective and a cop. Perhaps you should leave."

"Well, Popovich, we aren't in your country," I said.

I waited for a response as Popovich sized me up. Behind him, the gym reverberated with a symphony of sounds. Zzt, zzt, zzt came from the corner where shadow boxers punched at dead air. The chirping of jump ropes creasing the floor mixed with the sounds of hard punches finding flesh. Leather gloves striking heavy leather bags. Bang, bang, bang from the speed bag as it slammed against the backstop. Loud, brutal sounds. If perspiration had a sound, it would be here.

Popovich grunted. "You just missed Silva," he said. He came here with bruised knuckles and bloodied hands. I don't like this man. He brings a bad taste to my mouth. I had him thrown out."

"Julio Silva doesn't throw out easily," I said.

Popovich puffed his chest out like a proud father. "Edgar takes care of him."

"And who is Edgar?" I asked.

Popovich threw a thumb over his shoulder, pointing to the ring behind him. A black fighter his bronze skin glistening with sweat traded jabs with a white fighter. The white fighter was much shorter than his opponent. He tried burrowing his way inside to work the body of the taller man, but whenever he made a move, the taller man rocked him with a stiff jab. The bell rang, sending the fighters to their corners.

"That be Edgar," Popovich said. "As I was saying to you, Mr. Joe Caruso, perhaps you too should leave."

CHAPTER 6

I didn't argue with Alex Popovich, or did I want an agruement with Edgar. I hauled my butt back into the taxi and made a full circle winding up at the Daily Newspaper building. The evening was dwindling past the cocktail hour and Katrina was hungry. We grabbed a quick bite to eat at a nearby bar and grill. Eating bowls of chili on a warm evening didn't seem right, but bottles of cold beer set the temperature right. After dining we decided to visit Doctor Brooks Herrington.

We arrived at Herrington's two-story greystone in the glitzy Bleacher Hills neighborhood a few minutes before eight o'clock. Patio lights and a strong street lamp illuminated the yard. I swung open the gate to a waist-high wroth iron fence that surrounded the property. A cobblestone pathway led to the front door of the house. An alternative sidewalk marked by a small metal sign pointed the way to Doctor Herrington's office located on the lower level of the house. Katrina tried knocking a response on the residential door while I tested the office.

The office door was unlocked, so I walked inside. I flipped the wall switch that turned on the lights. The waiting room was modestly furnished. Four beige colored chairs lined one wall, and two floor lamps that provided light when the need called hugged opposite corners. The walls were painted an antiseptic white color like a hospital. It gave the room an uneasy cold feel.

The other room was larger than the first again conservatively furnished, but more comfortable in appearance from the muted earth tone colors of the walls and carpet that gave the room a relaxed feel. An executive desk almost hidden away in a corner stayed invisible from the two chairs in the middle of the room. One a reclining chair.

"No one is home," Katrina said, joining me. "Holy cow, do you smell that?" she asked.

"Smell what?" I said.

"The air smells clean," she said.

Katrina was right. The air smelled fresh and new, like a model home does when you first walk inside.

We walked through the rooms. Katrina running a fingertip across the furniture.

"Not a speck of dust," she said. She kicked the wastebasket. "Or crumbled papers in the basket. Either Doctor Herrington is a neat freak, or he seldom uses his office. Maybe this guy isn't real."

Katrina spoke into something no larger than a pack of cigarettes she held in her hand.

"What's that thing you're talking into?" I asked.

Katrina held it up. "This is a portable battery operated recorder," she said. "All of the television reporters in California are using them. I picked this one up when I lived there. Sure beats scripting notes."

"Can I get one of those?"

"Sure, I'll get you one," she said.

Four small stores occupied a strip of land across the street from Herrington's house. One store sold greeting cards, another women's clothing, a third was vacant and the forth a offered coffee. We retreated to the coffee shop to wait for Doctor Herrington to show. That was if there was a Doctor Herrington.

The coffee shop was claustrophobic. A short counter and clusters of tiny square tables with pastel-colored chairs packed into a space no larger than a thumb nail. We sat at a table by a window with a view of Herrington's place. Katrina pushed aside a finger vase of wilting flowers that obstructed the window.

A waitress handed out paper menus. She was of college-age with cropped dark hair, an ample bosom, and a thin waist. The off the wall café served flavored coffees and pawned dry muffins off as health food. We ordered hazelnut coffee and blueberry muffins. Taking up the menus, the waitress winked at Katrina before walking off.

"Have you notice how young women don't pay me any attention," I said.

"You have me, and I'm young," Katrina said.

I shrugged.

"Say your next words very carefully, Joe," Katrina warned.

The waitress came with our muffins and coffee. The coffee came in two of the biggest cups I've ever seen. She put them down on the table. Again she winked at Katrina.

"What did I tell you?" I said

Two gigantic cups of coffee later, we watched Phyllis Steele walk into Doctor Herrington's office. I felt like an unsuccessful angler fishing all day with no bites, and finally hooking a six-pound bass. I paid for the coffee, and Katrina and I jogged across the street.

We caught Mrs. Steele, sitting on one of the beige chairs in the waiting room. She looked uncomfortable, seeing me.

"Your instructions were to phone Doctor Herrington not show up at his office unannounced," she said, sounding annoyed. "Who is she?" She pointed at Katrina.

"She is Katrina Warring," I said.

"The newspaper reporter?" she snapped.

"In the flesh," I said. "And in a gather sexy red mini dress and matching high heel pumps."

"Are you always rude, Mr. Caruso?"

"Hey sweetheart, what happened to Joe, can I call you Joe and you can call me Phil? Where did that Phyllis Steele go?"

"I paid you to find Julio Silva," she said. "Do you have news about where he is?"

"No, I'm afraid I do not have any news. But what I'm confused about, Phil, if I may call you Phil, is why you want me to find Julio Silva?"

She stood, turned her back on me, and then spun on her heels to face me again. They were nice looking high heeled shoes. Expensive.

"You don't need to know why I want him found. Just find him," she said.

"Considering that I put Julio Silva, or should I say Julio Savona's sister in jail, I do need to know."

She sat back down and stared at the floor for a second, arranging her thoughts to what to say next.

"I don't want to read in your column, Miss Warring, what I'm about to tell you," she said, looking straight at Katrina.

"Can't promise that," Katrina said.

Phyllis leaned back in the chair and let loose with a deep sigh. "What the hell," she said. "My relationship with Julio was bound to come out." She shifted to the edge of the chair. "I'm frightened of him, Joe. I'm frightened what Julio might do to my husband and me."

She reached into the same purse she carried while in my office. She handed me a letter.

"I received this before I came to see you. It's from Julio."

I read the short note out loud. "I'm out of stir, baby. I never forgot you or your husband and what you did to me."

That was all it said.

"You had better start from the beginning," I said.

Phyllis took a deep breath. "Julio was a boxer. My husband and Jerry Pascoe co-managed his career. Jerry and Edward made Julio throw a fight."

"They bet against him?" I said.

Phyllis brushed a tear away from her eyes. "Yes, they told Julio to take a dive. He was ranked in the top five of heavyweight fighters. But he had no choice but to throw that fight. He was mad. Very mad, and later that night, Julio beat up a man."

"I know about the jail time," I said. "But what's your stake in all of this?"

She took another deep breath. "I loved Julio. Before I married Edward, Julio and I had a relationship."

"Now that Silva is out of jail, you think he wants to even the score with your husband," I said.

"Not just with Edward, but with anyone connected to him," Phyllis said.

"Does that include you?" I asked.

"Yes," she said.

CHAPTER 7

I'm not a morning person. All of that nonsense about the early bird catching the worm doesn't appeal to me. So when the alarm went off at eight o'clock, I turned it off and closed my eyes. When I finally rolled out of bed, the time was close to noon.

I showered and shaved. I found fresh clothes to wear and stepped outside to greet another day. A single storm cloud perched over Lake Michigan shifted inland overnight. It dropped buckets of rain that moistened the dry, cracked earth and washed winter's dirt off the sidewalks. The ground soaked up every drop of rainwater like a thirsty sponge. And then the rain stopped, and the sun re-emerged. In Chicago, the weather

changes faster than the second hand of a clock.

I started walking. Walking is not my preferred source of

transportation. But every so often, usually, in Spring, when the

air is fresh and clean, the birds come out singing, and the

temperature reaches above the sixty degrees mark my feet get

the itch to hit the pavement.

I spotted a welcoming café. A sign in its window promised a

juicy cheeseburger and cold beer for $2.95. I went inside and

took a seat at the counter. The waitress, a frail middle-aged

woman with broom straw hair and muscle less arms that

poked out from the half sleeves of a faded sunflower yellow

dress worn below a damp blue smock, took my order. I took

her up on the juicy burger and cold beer the menu offered. She

passed me the Sunday edition of the Daily News left orphaned

at the restaurant two days ago. I unraveled the paper to the cartoon section while waiting for my order I read Dick Tracy

when Shakespeare sat down beside me. Without looking, I

knew it was him. The smell of his cigar gave him away.

"How did you find me here?" I asked.

Shakespeare rebalanced his bottom on the too-small stool.

"You've been here before," he said. "Many times before, or

don't you remember?"

My order came. The waitress looked at Shakespeare, but he

waved her off. I took a bite of the cheeseburger, and then it hit

me. Katrina and I lunched here before.

Shakespeare reached to my plate and pulled off a potato chip.

"You know that guy you asked me about?"

"What guy?" I said.

"Herrington," he said.

I took another bite of the cheeseburger and washed it down

with a swallow of beer.

Shakespeare helped himself to another potato chip. "I got him locked up in a cell." He popped the chip into his mouth.

"What did he do?" I asked.

"Killed some rich dame. Got into a fight with her and messed her up good."

Shakespeare looked at the plate of chips. I nodded, and he took a handful.

"This dame's name wouldn't be Phyllis Steele, would it?" I took a bite out of the burger.

"That's the dame," Shakespeare said, pushing chips one at a time into his mouth. "You know her?"

"She was my client."

Shakespeare patted me on my back. "Well, buddy, I hope you got paid in advance."

CHAPTER 8

Brooks Herrington didn't look distinguished with his shirt open at the collar with his necktie missing, his slacks without a belt, and his oxford shoes minus their laces. Shakespeare did not want Herrington to hang himself with a six-inch shoelace or his belt, so he had them removed.

I pinched a cigarette through the bars. Herrington came over to grab it. He propped it between his lips and waited for me to light it with a match.

"I'm not talking until my lawyer gets here," Herrington said.

He took a toke off the cigarette and blew the smoke in my face.

"Relax, I'm not a cop," I said. "I'm a private detective. My name is Joe Caruso. Phyllis Steele was my client."

"I didn't kill Phyllis."

"The police seem to think you did," I said. "They found her body in your office. Hell, Herrington, I saw Mrs. Steele there yesterday evening. When I left, she stayed behind, waiting for you."

"What were you doing in my office?"

"Phyllis gave me your name as a contact," I said. I produced his business card, holding it up for him to see. "Cute little card you have there, Doc."

"What do you want from me?" he asked.

"Answers," I said.

"What makes you think I have anything to say that is of value to you?"

"You're the one sitting in this cell, so you tell me."

Herrington blew cigarette smoke from his nose. "I didn't kill Phyllis," he said.

People accused of murder aren't typically as brash as the doctor acted. Murder suspects act complacent, or scared, or remorseful. Herrington stayed combative, insisting that he didn't kill Phyllis Steele.

"I said, I'm not talking until my lawyer gets here," Herrington said. "Thanks for the smoke. Chesterfields are they? Not very Dunhill, are they?" Herrington dropped the cigarette and crushed it with the toe of his shoe and then marched back to the cot and sat down.

I went upstairs and sat in Shakespeare's office. The Lieutenant was at his desk with a large pizza in front of him.

"Are you going to eat that whole thing?" I asked.

"I was hungry," he said. "I missed breakfast."

"Breakfast was hours ago," I said.

"I'm making up for lost time, he said. "What did you pull out of the shrink?"

"Not much he swears he didn't kill Phyllis Steele."

"They all say that."

"I know, but I believe him," I said.

"What else did he say?"

"He doesn't like my brand of cigarette. Other than that, he's got lockjaw until his lawyer gets here."

I helped myself to a cup of coffee, took a sip of the java, but spit it out into the wastebasket. "When did you make this stuff?" I asked gagging.

Shakespeare shrugged his broad shoulders. "I don't know. Last week sometime. What, it's too strong?"

"Strong enough to kill a mule," I said. "Why can't a police station make a decent pot of coffee?"

"Beats me," Shakespeare said, reaching for another slice of pizza. "Maybe it's because we have better things to do."

"Like sitting around eating pizza," I said.

Shakespeare shoved the slice into his mouth. "Shut up," he muffled.

"Did you talk to the husband?" I asked.

"I told him his wife was dead," Shakespeare said.

"That's it?"

"What did you want me to ask him, how the weather was?"

"For starters, you should have asked him where he was at the time of the murder. Did he and his wife have marriage problems, or if anyone he knew carried a grudge against his wife."

"Why? We have the killed locked up in the basement, so why put the husband through all of that? He's had enough bad news for one day."

"How can you do this job day in and day out?" I asked.

"It's a living," Shakespeare said, using a paper napkin to wipe sauce off his mouth.

"If you're not going question, Mr. Steele, I will," I said.

Shakespeare shrugged. "Knock your socks off," he said.

CHAPTER 9

I stood on the sidewalk looking up at the apartment building where Edward and Phyllis Steele lived. Funny how every building in the ritzy Gold Coast neighborhood of Chicago looks bigger, cleaner, and more expensive than any of the other buildings in the city look. Who says money can't buy everything?

A security guard came out from the lobby to join me. He was young and handsome, with perfectly aligned white teeth and razor trimmed dusty brown hair plastered down with a sizable amount of hair cream. Broad shoulders filled in his pinstriped suit and a Van Heusen dress shirt tucked around a slender waist topped off his look, a look that screamed hours in a gym. More hours than at the kitchen table, that was for sure.

"She sure is something," he said.

"What's that?" I said.

"The building. She's a beauty."

"I guess so," I said. "I prefer blonds or brunettes with hour glass figures. But if bricks and plaster turn you on, so be it."

"Na, I dig dames too," the young guard said. "It's just that this here building is a beauty of Italian architecture. She's sleek and stylish like a good looking woman. I'm studying architecture at the community college." He spoke in quick stiletto sentences that were as sharp as the creases of his trousers. He paused and sucked in some air. "You have business here, fella, or just looking?"

"I came to see Mr. Steele, "I said.

"You one of those reporters?"

"Private detective." I handed him my business card.

"I had to ask. Those goons been here all morning." He glanced at the card. "Has Mr. Steele hired you, Mr. Caruso?"

"To be more precise, it was Mrs. Steele who hired me," I said.

He pocketed the card. "Too bad about the Mrs. She was a nice lady. Him, I don't care too much for. That's between you and me. Understood?" he underscored that last bit by poking a finger between my first and second rib.

"My lips stay sealed," I said.

"Good. As long as you and me see eye to eye, we'll get along."

He turned his back on me and pointed to the top floor of the building. My eyes followed his finger.

"The Steele's have the top floor penthouse," he said. "Seven bedrooms, three bathrooms, a formal dining room, formal living room, den, library, and gourmet kitchen all on ten thousand square feet of space with a bird's eye view of Lake Michigan."

I whistled. "Quite the pad."

"You ain't whistling Dixie," he said. "Pugs like you and me don't get to own digs like that. But my day is coming. You can bank that. Come on in; I'll show you to the express elevator."

The express elevator only went to the penthouse. The other snobs had to take the poor man's elevator. In less time than it took to count to six I stood on the tenth floor across from Edward Steele's penthouse apartment.

Before I could press the button for the doorbell, a woman opened the apartment door. She was tall, curvy, and blond.

"You must be psychic," I said.

"The security guard called ahead," she said.

Her voice hinted a Swedish accented and reminded me of cool nights sipping warm brandy, watching shooting stars streak across the Baltic sky.

"And I'm glad he did," I said.

"Is Mr. Steele expecting you, Mr. Caruso?"

I smiled. "And the guard also told you my name. And here I thought he and I were friends. And now that you know mine don't you think it is only proper that I know your name."

"Amelia Pendleton," she said.

Her name was stuffy. It didn't do her good looks justice.

"I couldn't have asked for a more delightful reception," I said, trying to melt the ice cycles that dripped from her voice.

"I asked you once and I will not ask again. Is Mr. Steele expecting you?" she said.

"No, but he'll want to see me. Mrs. Steele came by my office yesterday and hired me to track Julio Silva. I didn't get the chance. In some way, I feel I owe her."

"I'm sure you'll respect Mr. Steele's' wishes not to be disturbed. He is understandably distraught about his wife's death."

"Are you always so…cut and dry?" I asked.

"I can schedule a meeting on a future date," she said.

"Okay, if you're going to act that way, so can I. No, you may not schedule a meeting on a future date. What you can do is tell your boss that I insist on seeing him now."

"And if he refuses?"

"You can tell your boss about my dear friend, Katrina Warring. She writes a column for the Daily Newspaper. One call from me, and she will bring out every sleazy bit of gossip about Mrs. Steele that she can find. What do you think he'll want to do? Talk to me or read every juicy detail of his wife's dirty laundry in the evening edition."

Miss Pendleton pressed her lips tight together. "I'll talk to Mr. Steele." She turned on her heels and walked out of sight down a hallway.

CHAPTER 10

What I knew about Edward Steele could fit at the bottom of a shot glass. I knew the man had money. So much money he could afford a classy penthouse overlooking Lake Michigan, and a good looking wife who bought up a good chunk of the Magnificent Mile. Judging by the outrage I heard coming from the back of the apartment, I'd say that Steele also owned a hot temper.

Miss Pendleton came back. Her fixed expression not changed from the episode with Steele.   "Please excuse the yelling," she said modestly. "Mr. Steele is extremely distressed."

Distressed nothing. I'd say that Edward Steele was coming unglued. But Miss Pendleton was a trouper. She showed no break in her polished disposition as she showed me to a room where I waited.

In a short time, Edward Steele showed up. He wasn't at all what I expected. My mental picture of Steele cast a short, stout man with pasty skin and tired eyes. Standing around six feet with a full-bodied physique, Edward Steele cast an impressive shadow for a middle-aged man. His clothes were casual-simple pants, a plaid shirt with the tail untucked. He wore no shoes or socks. He didn't look like a Gold Coast addressee, that was for sure. A ranch in Montana seemed more his style.

Barefooted he plodded across the thick beige wall to wall carpeting to an executive desk that occupied the premier location in front of two sets of French doors that opened to a private balcony. The desk was a mess. The balcony was not.

"You got five minutes," he said.

"My name is Joe Caruso," I started to say.

"I know who you are," he said. "Miss Pendleton told me. You're a detective my wife hired. I'll cut to the chase, Mr. Caruso. You're barking up the wrong tree if you're looking for more money. Whatever funds my wife paid you is what you'll get. Your contract was with her and not with me."

"Your wife hired me to track down Julio Silva," I said.

Steele got up and walked to a bar made from a couple of well-positioned shelves. He selected a bottle of whiskey and poured himself a drink. He didn't offer me whiskey, or a cigar which he helped himself to next, or a chair to sit in as he returned to his chair behind his desk.

"I know about you and Julio Silva," I said.

Like a man lost in the desert, Steele drank his drink in one gulp. He brushed his mouth dry, using the back of his hand.

"I sponsored Julio. Me, and Jerry Pascoe. Did you ever see Julio fight?"

I shook my head, no.

"He was beautiful. He was a true heavyweight. He had a punch like a pile driver. Jerry and I had high hopes for Julio. Heavyweight champion hopes."

"What happened?" I asked.

Steele's eyes stretched to the back of his head. He recalled memories that weren't good. "There was this fighter. Max Kowalski. A real powder-puff, but connected, so he won a lot of fights. All fixed mind you. The night he was fighting Julio, Jerry came to tell us that Julio had to lose. The betting line was for a knockout in the fifth round. Julio had to take the fall. Julio didn't like it, but he had no choice."

"You made Julio take a dive."

Steele shrugged. "As I said, we had no choice. The fix was in."

"So you and Pascoe bet against your fighter."

"What else should we have done? Jerry and I were in the game to make money, not friends. We rook care of Julio. He got his taste."

"And later that night he got into a bar brawl, beat up some guy and got tossed in jail. You really took care of him."

Steele pointed his finger at me. "You got no right to judge me, Caruso. I give more to this city than anyone."

"And Julio goes to jail for five years," I said.

"It was for the boy's good. Julio is an animal."

"You don't think that Brooks Herrington killed your wife," I said. "You think it was Silva and you're scared."

"Silva is an animal. You'll find that out if he comes to you."

"Why was your wife seeing, Herrington?" I asked.

Edward Steele sank deep into the padding of his chair. All six feet of him deflated like an old balloon.

"She was sick," he said. "Phyllis was a stubborn woman. Headstrong, you might say if you knew her."

"Your wife told me that Herrington was treating her for a sexual disorder."

Steele narrowed his eyes at me. "Haven't you been listening? Phyllis was sick.

Edward Steele said he would give me five minutes, and five minutes was what I got. Precisely at the appointed time Miss. Pendleton came into the room, ready to escort me out.

CHAPTER 11

Shakespeare was leaning against the building, smoking a cigar, and blowing smoke rings. A cool breeze blew the smoke rings across Michigan Avenue. They grew wider and thinner as they traveled. Crossing the Magnificent Mile, they became transparent, floating away like ghosts.

"Don't you have a murder scene to visit," I said.

I stood at the edge of the sidewalk, looking both ways for a vacant taxi. There were none. I fished in a pocket for my Chesterfields.

"You see one dead body stuffed inside a trash can you've seen them all," Shakespeare said, stepping away from the building.

I put one of the cigarettes into my mouth. Shakespeare flicked his lighter and lit it. I sucked in the smoke and blew it out the corner of my mouth.

"You could have come up and said hello to Ed Steele," I said.

"No need. I have you," he said.

Shakespeare returned his hand to his pocket. Hunched his shoulders as if he felt chilled.

"You are one stubborn son of a you know what, Caruso," he said.

We watched traffic zoom by on Michigan Avenue.

"Your case died with Phyllis Steele," Shakespeare said. "Why don't you take the fifty or whatever, the dollars she paid you and treat your pretty girlfriend to dinner?"

"Dead or alive, Phyllis Steele is still my client," I said.

"Like I said, stubborn."

Shakespeare kicked a stone into the street.

"My bet is your next move is a visit with our new medical examiner, Doctor Peterson. Am I right?"

"Are you planning on following me?" I asked.

Shakespeare shook his head. "No, I'm not following you, I'm driving you."

Shakespeare parked his unmarked police car at the curb next to a fire hydrant. A parking ticket fluttered in the breeze under the wiper blade. Shakespeare pulled it off and tossed it into the gutter. He folded his big frame into the driver's seat, and I got into the passenger seat. We were on our way to Cook County Hospital.

"I miss old Doc Samuels," Shakespeare said. "This new Doc is colder than the stiffs in her iceboxes?"

Doctor Samuels, the City's resident medical examiner, retired after forty years on the job. Until tonight I had no occasion to meet his replacement, Irene Peterson. I heard she was a hard-nosed professional. If true, that meant that Peterson and Shakespeare would soon butt heads.

Doctor Peterson met us in the corridor outside the examination room. Irene Peterson was a tall, slender woman of fifty years of age. Her dark hair was pushed back and showed the slightest tinge of gray. Her eyes were cold, steel blue. I imagined her personality to be the same.

"I haven't performed an autopsy, but I can safely say that Mrs. Steele died from blunt force trauma to the body and head. I will venture to say this. By the look of her, I'd say that someone beat Mrs. Steele with a baseball bat."

"Could her injuries have come from punches?" I asked

"I don't know. Possibly," Peterson said. "But the punches would have had to have been severe."

"Could a boxer do that much damage?" I asked. "You know, a professional prizefighter. Could a professional fighter hit so hard to rupture internal organs?"

"Yes," Peterson said.

CHAPTER 12

"There's no way Brooks Herrington could have done that much damage to Phyllis Steele's body to cause her death," I said to Shakespeare. "You've seen the guy. He's a toothpick."

We were walking side by side down the corridor aiming for the exit door.

"Toothpicks have sharp ends," Shakespeare said, pushing open the door and stepping outside. "He might have gone looney on her."

"I don't think he has it in him," I said.

"That's your opinion. I say different. Anyway, his lawyer sprung him. Herrington is probably at home toasting freedom with champagne."

"Did you catch the lawyer's name?"

"Nah. Why, do you need a good mouthpiece?'

We were walking down the sidewalk that wound up in the

parking lot.

"What did I tell you about Peterson," Shakespeare said.

"She's a cold fish."

"A cold fish can thaw," I said.

Shakespeare chuckled. We're all full of metaphors today,

aren't we?

At the car Shakespeare stopped short of opening his door.

"Where do you want me to drop you?" he asked.

"I'll catch a taxi," I said.

He nodded, got into his car, and drove off.

Flagging down a taxi is a skill. Hailing a ride isn't as easy as

sticking your hand in the air. 80% of fares are businessmen.

They're good tippers. The other 20% are good looking

women. So, where does that leave a guy like me? With a fighter's chance at best.

Call it luck, but I managed to catch a taxi on my first try even if I had to step out into the middle of the street, coming close to being run over by the cab. But like a batter stepping into a fastball to get on first base-it was worth the try.

My good luck taxi ride came to a grinding stop in rush hour. At the rate the traffic was moving, I was a solid hour away from home. My stomach cried for food. I got out of the cab and walked. I spotted Lawry's Restaurant, The Prime Rib, a block down the street. The perfect place for dinner.

Lawry's is one of Chicago's many legendary restaurants. Celebrities travel from near and far to eat in the converted old McCormick mansion. All come for the food, but a few come for the hauntings.

The McCormick family of McCormick spice fame lived a grandiose lifestyle in the house that is now Lawry's restaurant. Rumors of ghostly appearances began after a cleaning man called police at two o'clock in the morning scared out of his mind. He swore that he saw the ghost of Mr. McCormick walking the eatery. Since then many more folks claimed to have seen the ghost of old man McCormick. The prospect of seeing a phantom while dining on a medium-rare filet of beef interested some people. Others were not so impressed.

I never saw the ghost. At least not while sober.

I sat at the bar and used the telephone to call Katrina. Her story about the Phyllis Steele murder had her bogged down, making deadline a nightmare to achieve. She promised to meet me for breakfast.

I stayed at the bar and had a dinner of prime rib hand-carved to order and baked potato washed down by several dirty martinis.

After dinner, I took a taxi home but got out at the corners of Park and Lexington. The night was warm with a gentle breeze, so I walked home from there.

Home and office are the same — two connecting rooms on the fourth floor of a building whose architect should have done prison time for designing the building. It leans to the north. If I put a pencil down at one end of my desk, it rolls to the other end.

The landlord should also be in jail for being a slumlord. The lobby floor dirty from years of unwashed grim has cracked linoleum in several spots near the doors and stairs. Every other day the elevator stops working, and the burned-out light bulbs in the hallways need changing.

I lost count if today was a good or bad day for riding the elevator. I kept my fingers crossed that today was one of the good days and didn't uncross them until I stepped out onto my floor.

The door to my office was ajar. That in itself isn't a cause for alarm. Sometimes I leave it unlocked. If a prospective client comes by he, or she could wait inside. Of course, that does entice the occasional burglar, but I haven't that much to steal. Thieves are welcome to the old cuckoo clock. The cuckoo flew the coop years ago.

I walked into the room and saw the outline of a big man sitting in the darkness. I heard his breathing before I saw his face.

"You Caruso?" the man asked.

He had a deep voice. An unpleasant voice.

"I have a message for Caruso," he said. Air snorted from his nose when he spoke as if he was having trouble breathing.

"I'm Caruso," I said.

He stood and clumped across the floor, puffing along the way, and stopped too close for my comfort.

"Okay, buster," I said. "So, what's your message?"

He welded a fist out of an oversized hand. "This," he said and hit me.

CHAPTER 13

When my eyes opened, I saw the big man was sitting in the same chair he sat in when I came in. He was biting on his fingernails to keep busy. I reached under my jacket for my gun. I grabbed air.

"It ain't there," the big man said. "Your gun. It ain't there. I took it. I took the one in the desk drawer too."

I struggled to my feet. "Those weapons are expensive hardware."

"I stashed them in the filing cabinet," he said. "Now, you have something in there to look forward to getting out."

I limped to my desk and sat down, putting my desk between him and me.

"I guess you're Julio Silva," I said.

"Savona," the man said.

I shrugged. "Savona, Silva, what's in a name. You're the same guy, an ex-heavyweight who got a raw deal." I massaged my jaw. "Prison didn't dull you. You still pack a decent punch."

"That was the appetizer," he said.

"In that case, I'll pass on the entrée," I said.

I brought out the office bottle of bourbon and two coffee mugs, dumping the day-old coffee in one mug into the wastebasket. I poured whiskey in both cups and slid one cup to the big man. He scooted his chair over to the desk to take the cup. I watched it disappear in his hand.

"What are you doing here?" I asked. "The police want to talk to you about Mr. Ore and Phyllis Steele. They think you might know something about their deaths."

"Who thinks that?"

"Me for one."

"But you're not saying anything, are you?"

"Why did Phyllis Steele want you found," I said. "Why, Julio? What did you have on the lady that made her fear you?"

He stared me down with dark eyes barely visible through the thick scar tissue around them.

"I loved Phil," he said in a strange, haunting voice.

"Now that we're chatting like two friends sitting on a park bench, convince me that you didn't kill Phyllis Steele.

He pounded his fist on the desk. I jumped along with everything on the desk.

"I said I loved her."

"You have a strange way of showing affection," I said.

He fell back into the chair, letting his shoulders sag. "Phil and me were good," he said.

He drifted away, thinking about the days when he had the world by the horns. Good days until his world got turned inside out. Now he looked peaceful, and I didn't want to jolt him out of his euphoria. God only knew what Julio would do to me if I did. So, I let him rest.

"They spoiled things," he finally said.

"Who?" I asked.

"All of them," he answered. "Ed and Jerry, my managers. The lawyer, the judge, and Phil. Phil left me cold turkey."

As he spoke, his face distorted into an ugly mask of scar tissue, and injury. The muscles of his arms tightened. His muscles hadn't turned to fat while in jail. He still looked like he could go ten rounds in the ring without catching a breath.

"Ed and Jerry screwed me," Julio said, pushing his glass to me for a refill. "They made me throw that fight that was mine to win. I was one stinking win away from a title fight. A big payday. But instead of me getting the championship belt wrapped around my waist, I got this."

He stood, tugged at the belt around his waist, pulling it through the pant loops.

"It's a cardboard belt. That's what you get from prison. Instead of me getting a big fight in a stadium, I go to prison and get a cardboard belt. What luck, huh?"

He sat back down, grabbed the glass, and I saw the anger in his eyes. He looked like a big cat that wanted nothing more than to rip the lungs out of his prey.

"They did that to me: Jerry and Ed, people I trusted. But the worse came from Phil. She said that she loved me. She screwed me too."

"I'm sorry, Julio, but the past is the past," I said.

He pointed a thick finger at me. "You screwed me too. You put my sister Maria in jail. I want you to get my sister, Maria, out of the slammer."

"How am I to do that?"

"You put her there. Now you get her out."

"Be reasonable, Julio, your sister, is serving time for manslaughter."

"She didn't do it."

"The evidence all pointed to her," I said.

"Jerry Pascoe killed Light Fingers."

"And how do you know that Pascoe killed Domenic Conte?"

"I shared a cell with Tony Conte Domenic's kid brother. He told me."

"Jail cell confessions are a hard sell to a judge. I'll need more than that to go on."

"You get Maria out of jail," he thundered.

"And what happens if I say no?"

He clenched his hand in a fist and held it in front of my face.

"I'll hit you until you say yes."

"You make a convincing argument," I said.

"I've got money," he said.

Julio reached into his pocket and brought out a wad of money that a horse could choke on. He peeled off two hundred dollars in twenty-dollar bills as easy as if he were dealing cards. He dropped the money on the desk and stood to leave.

"I'll be back in two days," he said. "By then, you should have some idea on how to spring Maria."

"And what if I don't?" I asked.

"Then you should hold on to the two hundred bucks. It will pay for a doctor or an undertaker whichever comes first."

"What about Phyllis?" I said.

The outside street light came in through the window. It

flowed over Julio's face, chest and arms, and he said.

"Forget about her. I have." And he walked away.

CHAPTER 14

My memory of the Conte case was Foggy. Too many years, too many drinks and too many knocks to the noggin passed since then. I needed a refresher, but I didn't dare call Shakespeare.

Pulling him away from a good night's sleep would be a significant setback to my physical health. So, I called Pepper Marlow, the one person I knew I could bother at this time of the night.

When Pepper Marlow retired from the police force he bought O'Bannon's Tavern, a cop bar, in Edison Park, a cop neighborhood. If Pepper didn't know anything about Conte, he could find out. All he had to do was yell across the barroom full of cops. Somebody would answer.

"Jerry Pascoe?" Pepper said. "That's a name I haven't heard in a long time. Pascoe and Conte, now that's old school, Joey. What are you in to now?"

I told Pepper about Julio Savona's visit. His claim that Pascoe killed Conte and not Maria, his sister.

"The Conte case didn't pass my desk until the very end of my stay in homicide," I said. "The case belonged to Eddie Fudge, my former partner. Eddie handled it without me."

Pepper said. "If I recall, you stayed two sheets under the wind too many days back then."

Pepper was right. Back in the days when I worked homicide, I never passed up a bottle to call my friend. Working murder is a terrible business. Most detectives fall back on something to keep their heads on straight. My vice was booze.

"Sure, I can help you out," Pepper said. "I can sniff around, but I'll need something in return. Come on by the bar, and I'll tell you what it is I need."

"I'll be there tomorrow," I said.

"What's wrong with coming by tonight?"

"It's late."

"The bar is open until late."

I sighed. "I was hoping to get some sleep."

I could hear Pepper smirk. "You can sleep once you're dead. And in your case, that day might come sooner than later."

CHAPTER 15

O'Bannon's Tavern serves beer and whiskey. No wine, or martinis, and no gimlets. Entertainment was a pool table and a dartboard. There might be a jukebox, but I never heard it play. But no one came to O'Bannon's for entertainment. O'Bannon's was a place where retired and active cops went to get drunk. Let off some steam.

The clock chimed midnight, the enchanting hour when I steered my bone-weary body through the doors of O'Bannon's. The late hour thinned the regular inebriated clientele to seven. Four slumped over the bar and three arguing over a dart game. Pepper poured me a beer from the tap and pointed at a table in the back of the room.

The son of an Irish cop, Pepper, looked the clone of his dad-short legs and a long torso, close-set hazel colored eyes, long narrow nose, and reddish-brown hair. Pepper logged twenty years on the police force. He never made it to detective because, in his words, he hated wearing a suit and tie.

Pepper sat down. He leaned across the table to get closer to me.

"It's like this," Pepper said "I've been robbed. Fifteen hundred smackers, and I think one of my people did it."

I leaned back putting air between me and Pepper's Irish whiskey breath.

"How did that happen? Your people are tighter with money than British Bankers."

"Last week, one of my bartenders worked closing. I usually close the place, but that night I had to take the wife out on the town. You don't know how that is, Joe. You're one of the lucky ones without a ball and chain. Or maybe you're not that lucky. Anyway, I didn't think nothing of Rocco closing. He's done it before. There's not much to it. Lock the door, clean up a little, count the money in the cash drawer, and then put it into a bank bag, carry the bag to the bank and drop it in the night deposit. A monkey could do it. If I could find a monkey, I'd give it a job. The next morning, I go to the bank, and there's no deposit. I question Rocco, and he says he made the deposit just as always."

"So you figure that your bartender didn't make the drop or someone at the bank palmed the cash," I said.

Pepper nodded. "That's my take."

"So, what is it you want me to do, Pepper?" I asked.

"I'd be obliged if you could find out who robbed me, Joe," he said.

"You have a barroom filled with cops, Pepper. Why drag me here from across town when you could finger one of these guys to poke around for you."

"Most of these guys are retired. They would just as soon jump into a pit of snakes than work again. I'll look into the Conte thing for you if you snoop around and get back my lost dough. What do you say?"

"The old one hand washes the other hand. Right Pepper?"

"You said it, Joe. That's the Chicago way."

CHAPTER 16

It was two o'clock in the morning when I walked out of O'Bannon's Tavern. I went home and got into bed, hoping to get eight hours of sleep. I didn't. Katrina woke me at half-past seven.

Wake up sleepyhead," she said.

"How did you get in here?" I asked, still dopey from sleep.

"I have a key. Remember?"

"You should move in."

"Move in here?" she looked around the room. "Not on your life."

"But, I'm irresistible."

"Don't press your luck," she said.

My head fell back down on the pillow. The only thing worse than waking up with a hangover is waking up early in the morning with one. My head felt like it had been split open with a jackhammer. I didn't remember getting undressed, but there I was flat on my back wearing nothing but my boxer shorts and black socks.

"Get dressed, you're buying breakfast," Katrina said.

I sat up slowly, letting my brain settle. It teetered inside my skull like a loose marble. When the room stopped spinning, I stood and, with unsteady legs, walked to the bathroom. Splashing cold water on my face brought me back to life. Toothpaste and mouthwash washed away the awful residue of the beer and cheap whiskey I drank at O'Bannon's. A razor to whiskers and a comb through my hair, and I almost looked presentable. Now I needed coffee, and if I could stand looking at them a plate of scrambled eggs.

We walked down the block to Lou's Diner.

Lou wasn't at all sympathetic to my ill health. Today wasn't the first time I walked into his diner feeling under the weather, and it wouldn't be my last. He dropped the coffee cup down on the counter with a bang. He could have placed it down gracefully, but Lou had a funny streak. He enjoyed teasing me whenever I showed up miserable in the morning after the night before, so I didn't complain. But I lost my temper when he rattled the silverware in my ear, and I told him to quit. Telling a former navy guy like Lou to stop is like spitting into the wind.

The waitress brought me a tall glass of orange juice. The girl was new on the job. She didn't know I preferred tomato juice. I drank the orange juice anyway and found it so good I asked her for a second glass. I drank the juice and enough coffee to fill a longshoreman's thermos twice. I handled the drinks with no repercussions, but I retched seeing the plate of eggs. I pushed them aside and opted instead for a bowl of oatmeal with sliced bananas and dry toast.

Katrina wolfed down two over-easy eggs, bacon, and toast. I turned away, unable to look at the runny egg whites on her plate.

"Julio Silva paid me a visit last night," I said.

"And you're alive to tell about it," she said.

"I'm sure he killed Fredrick Ore and Phyllis Steele. He didn't say he did or didn't, but I got the impression from him that he had a bone to pick with both of them."

"Judge Fredrick Ore sentenced Silva to five years in prison," Katrina said. "Is that a good reason to kill him?"

"For some people that is."

"And Julio Silva is that type."

"Yes, he is."

"No wonder Phyllis Steele was frightened of him. She hired you to find him before he found her."

Katrina sipped coffee. My stomach growled indicating that my appetite returned.

"Why did he come to you?" Katrina asked.

"He wants me to get his sister, Maria out of jail. Julio claims Jerry Pascoe killed Domenic Conte, and not his sister."

"Interesting seeing that police found Maria in Conte's room with the murder weapon in her hand."

"Julio said Jerry Pascoe framed his sister."

"And pray tell where did Mr. Silva get this information? Did a carrier pigeon fly into his cell with a note strapped to its foot?"

"Tony Conte was Julio's cellmate."

"Domenic's brother?" Katrina said.

She ran a piece of toast across her plate, scooping up egg yolk. She shook her head in disbelief. "Tony Conte is a druggie. He can't be trusted to say what day it is."

The sound of sizzling bacon coming from Lou's griddle was making me hungry. I considered ordering bacon and eggs.

"What are you going to do?" Katrina asked.

She pushed her plate aside, picked up her coffee cup and peered at me over the rim of the cup waiting for my answer.

"You'd make a good shrink," I said. "I'll look into it."

The waitress came to our table to refill our cups. I ordered bacon and eggs. I asked her to tell Lou to crash the eggs.

"Allow me to paint a picture about what will happen when you tell Shakespeare that a murder suspect paid you a late night visit. And what did you do? You sat around drinking whiskey with him. After he pours out his heart to you you let him walk away. Is that the story you're going to give

Shakespeare?"

"Something like that," I said.

My order of bacon and eggs came.

"Shakespeare won't like it," Katrina said.

"Shakespeare cries over everything I do or say."

Katrina watched me eat. "Terrance Johnson was the city

prosecutor that charged Julio Silva with assault for that bar

fight. He also prosecuted Maria Savona."

I looked up from my plate.

"Judge Ore and Terrance Johnson are partners in a law firm

with Jacob Pendleton."

I held back a forkful of egg from going into my mouth.

"Amelia Pendleton is Edward Steele's girl Friday," I said. "So

what's he to Amelia? Her father or husband or just a name in

the phone book?"

"Her brother," Katrina said.

"Small world," I said.

"It's about to get smaller," she said. "Jacob Pendleton is

Edward Steele's attorney."

CHAPTER 17

"You just let him walk out of your office?" Shakespeare bellowed.

I was leaning against his office door. My legs crossed, and my hands deep inside my pockets I tried looking as relaxed as possible.

Katrina stood nearby, chewing a stick of bubble gum. Occasionally she blew a bubble.

Shakespeare paced like an angry tiger. Occasionally he growled.

"Did he have a gun to your head, or are you just that lame?"

Katrina said, "I told you that the Lieutenant wasn't going to be happy with you, Joe."

Shakespeare stopped putting his face close to her. He was looking at her but pointed a thick finger at me.

"You're darn tooting I'm not happy. I'm furious. I could jail your boyfriend for obstructing a murder investigation."

"You don't have enough evidence against Silva to ticket him for jaywalking," I said.

"Are you forgetting something, Caruso? There's a lady in the morgue that looks like someone used her for a punching bag. That's all the evidence I need."

"Aren't you curious why Julio Silva visited me?" I asked.

"I'll bite, why?"

"Because I arrested his sister for murder."

"And who pray tell is his sister?"

"Maria Savona."

"Silva is Julio's fighting name," Katrina said. "Julio's real name is Savona."

"I arrested his sister for the murder of Domenic Conte," I said.

"Let me guess," Shakespeare said. "His sister is innocent."

"That's what he came to tell me."

"Did he offer any suggestion as who did kill Conte? You understand that I'm being facetious."

"That's a big word," I said, looking at Katrina.

"A huge word," she said.

"Quit with the wisecracks," Shakespeare growled.

"Jerry Pascoe killed Domenic Conte," I said.

"Here's the good part, Lieutenant," Katrina said. "Go ahead, Joe, tell the Lieutenant the name of Silva's source."

"Tony Conte," I said.

"Domenic's loser brother?" Shakespeare said.

"Tony told Julio while the two shared a prison cell," I said.

Shakespeare let out a sigh that sounded like the air when you open a pickle jar. He dropped into his chair, leaned back, and loosened his necktie.

"I'm getting tired of this trash," he said. "There have been more murders this month than last month. And last month was higher than the month before, and it ain't even August." He lit a cigar. "Now you come in here telling me this stuff.

"The story gets deeper," Katrina said.

Shakespeare ran a hand across his forehead. "Does it get crazier?" he asked.

"You betcha it does," she said.

The cigar danced in Shakespeare's mouth. His bloodshot eyes asked for sleep, but the wheels behind them were turning too fast to stop. "I can't wait," Shakespeare said.

I told him the entire story.

CHAPTER 18

I took my leave of Katerina and Lieutenant Shakespeare to pursue Pepper Marlow's theft. The sooner I got that off the back burner, the better position I would be in to tackle what Phyllis Steele paid me to do in the first place, and that was to find Julio Silva. Granted, Silva found me before I could find him. And double granted, my client was dead. But I still felt an obligation to her. Now my task was finding her killer and putting him away.

I don't think straight standing around, so I walked around the neighborhood. After slumming down alleys and streets deserted with houses, I wound up at Eddie's Tavern- a hole in the wall bar that opened early to accommodate third shifters from nearby factories. On a beautiful sunlit spring, morning Eddies was smoky, cold and dim like a mausoleum. Wood walls painted over in uneven strokes of dark grey held photographs of men wearing plaid shirts holding stringers of fish and the heads of dead deer. A calendar featuring scantly dressed women hung by the door. I counter eight men, not counting the bartender, and one woman in the place. I straddled a stool at the very end of the bar.

When I walked in, the men stopped talking. They started up again after I sat down. They spoke in loud nasty voices arguing about baseball, politics, their union bosses, and anything else they could think about at this hour of the morning. They drank beer.

The bartender, a short, fat man, wiped down the bar top in front of me. He leaned over the bar getting closer to me. The pimples on his chin made him look like a warthog. His eyes droopy from overwork in the dim light of the tavern. He looked unhappy with life.

"You a cop?" he said, from the side of his mouth.

"Does it show?" I said.

"You ain't wearing an apron, so you ain't one of them," he said.

The eight men, third shifters from the nearby sausage packing house, all wore aprons under wool coats. Some aprons had bloodstains.

"And I don't believe you came in here for Lola."

Lola was the lady sitting at the other end of the bar. She was of an undetermined age, and wore a loose-fitting blouse with the top three buttons unhitched showing off a mature bosom that once must have been firm and gorgeous, but sagged today. Her blond hair looked a wreck, and she wore too much makeup. The woman sat alone, hoping to pick up a fast buck for a quickie out back.

"So you must be the law," the bartender said.

"Do you have bourbon?" I asked.

The bartender pointed to bottles lined up on the shelve above the cash register. "No good stuff," he said. "The best is rotgut."

"Then rotgut it is," I said.

He stepped on a stool to reach for a bottle. Wiped the neck before pulling the cork. He poured the booze halfway into a dusty glass. I drank two before leaving. Lola wasn't at the end of the bar when I went. I counted seven men.

The transition from being inside a dark tavern to moving outside in broad daylight can be challenging without wearing sunglasses. The sunlight hit me like an atomic explosion. I shielded my eyes as I walked down the sidewalk to the corner and a waiting taxi.

The driver was reading a Playboy magazine. He had the playmate of the month folded out over the steering wheel. "Just look at those jugs," he said joyfully. "Man, oh man, if my wife had jugs like those, I'd never leave home." He kissed the centerfold and then folded up his magazine. "Where to mister?"

I gave him Jimmie Rocco's address on Franklin Street. A ritzy neighborhood near the Hyatt Hotel. A luxury not many a six-year cop on disability and with a gambling problem could afford.

Rocco liked shooting dice, but his rolls always turned up snake eyes. So his expensive address had me worried.

I rolled down the window to let the air cool me off. I thought about sticking my head out the window like a dog, but I didn't. The ride was much shorter than I wanted it to be. I was still slightly under the weather from rotgut bourbon when we pulled to a stop outside Jimmie Rocco's apartment building. I climbed out of the cab, paid the driver, and walked into the building and up the stairs to Jimmie's apartment. I was sober by the time I hit the third floor. I knocked on the door.

Rocco was on a six-month disability vacation after getting shot in the leg. I waited for him to open the door.

"Hi there, Caruso," Jimmie said, yawning. "I haven't seen you in a coon's age. What brings you here?"

Jimmie Rocco had lost weight from last I saw him. So much lost weight that his rib cage showed under his tee-shirt. His belt pinched on the last notch was still having trouble holding his pants up. His hair was greasy. His face dry. His eyes bloodshot.

"How's the leg, Jimmie," I said, letting myself inside.

"I'm still wobbling around, but I get by," said Jimmie closing the door and limping up behind me. "Say, what are you doing here?"

"You know why I'm here, Jimmie," I said, casing the apartment. It was a nice apartment-clean with modern furniture and light coming in the windows.

"No, I don't," Jimmie said with a shrug.

"How many rooms do you have here?" I asked. "Four, five? Two bedrooms? How much does the rent set you back each month? Where is Pepper's money?"

"I don't know what you're talking about, Joe."

"Don't play me for a fool, Jimmie. I know you swiped Pepper's dough."

"Hey, I would never do such a thing to Pepper. You know me, Joe, I'm on the up and up."

"Yeah, I know you, Jimmie. You're as up and up as a lead balloon. You'd steel a blind man blind. Now, where is Pepper's money?"

Jimmie ran a hand through his hair, pushing it down over his head. The other hand scratched inside the waistband of his pants. He sat down on the sofa, spread his legs wide, and dropped his head between his knees like he was looking to the floor for his car keys.

"I'm over the 8-ball, Joe. I owe big time, and if I don't come up with the dough, I'm going to get bumped off. I didn't want to steal from Pepper, he's been good to me, but I had no choice."

"So, the money is gone?"

"No, I still got it. Tomorrow I'm supposed to meet and turn it over."

"Give it to me."

"If I do that, I'm a dead man."

"That's your problem, Jimmie. Give me the money. You know I'm walking out of here with Pepper's money. It's your decision, how."

Jimmie pointed to the closet at the far side of the room. "It's in the closet. In that duffle bag."

I found the duffle bag, opened it to make sure the money was in there and headed for the door.

"I'm a dead man, Joe. You signed my death certificate."

"No, Jimmie, you signed your death certificate by screwing around with the odds."

"Tell Pepper I'm sorry. Will you do that for me, Joe?"

"You tell him yourself," I said, grabbing Jimmie by the neck. "Get some clothes on; you're coming with me."

CHAPTER 19

There were more cops in O'Bannon's then at City Hall on Labor Day weekend. From behind the bar, Pepper nudged his head to a table at the back of the barroom. Jimmie and I took chairs there and waited.

"What will Pepper do to me?" Jimmie asked, his hands shaking nervously.

Not being reassuring, I said, that was for Pepper to decide.

"I was going to pay him back. Honest, I was."

"Tell that to Pepper," I said.

Jimmie dropped his face into his hands. He started to sob.

"I'm screwed," he whispered.

Pepper came to the table and sat down across from Jimmie. He gave Jimmie that damned if you do and damned if you don't look.

Jimmie started to tell Pepper how sorry he was, but Pepper stopped him.

"Don't tell me how sorry you are. Don't say anything. I'll do the talking you do the listening. You're a good guy, Rocco," Pepper said calmly. "But you have a weakness. We all have weaknesses. You should know all about that, Joe."

"This isn't about me, Pepper," I said, "it's between you and Jimmie. Either turn the other cheek, or hang him out to dry, but leave me out of it."

Jimmie's eyes grew wide as saucers. "Wait one minute," he said, taking hold of my wrist. "You're not going to let him drag me out back?"

I pulled Jimmie's hand off me. "You ripped Pepper off. So the way I see it is whatever Pepper deems appropriate retribution, then so be it.

What happened next depended on Pepper's state of mind. Was he in an eye for an eye mood or a forgiving mood? Truthfully? I didn't care one way or the other. Pepper could take Rocco to the river and toss him in for all I cared. I had my problems to worry about.

Pepper crossed his arms on the table. "As I was saying, we all have weaknesses, and gambling is yours." Pepper shook his head. "I'm not happy with you, Jimmie. Not happy at all."

"This will make you happy," I said to Pepper handing him Jimmie's duffle bag with the fifteen hundred dollars inside.

Pepper unzipped the bag and counted out the money as Jimmie explained why he stole the tavern's receipts. Jimmie surprised me for not making any excuses. He spoke to Pepper man to man fessing up to the thief. Sometimes telling the truth works and other times it doesn't.

"I'll talk to Patty, on your behalf, Jimmie," Pepper said. "I'll buy your marker. For me, she'll settle for two bits on the dollar."

"Who is Patty?" I asked. "I know every bookie in town, but I never heard of a dame named Patty."

"Patty is the Fisher Queen," Pepper said. "Patty Fisher is new in town. She deals ponies and dice strictly."

"Soft money bets are a hard crawl to the top," I said.

"Patty has the legs for it," Pepper said.

"A real doll baby," I said.

Pepper smirked. "A doll baby with a pearl-handled revolver and two bodyguards with more muscle than a New Zealand Rugby team.

I whistled. "You are a lucky bloke, Jimmie. You should kiss Pepper's ring. He's your Pope."

Jimmie Rocco swallowed hard. "Thanks, Pepper," he mumbled.

"You're not getting off scot-free," Pepper said. "You'll have to pay some price, Rocco. She'll go light. A couple of punches to the gut, even a broken finger, is better than wearing a dirt overcoat. Thank your lucky stars it isn't worse. Now, get lost. I have business to talk over with Joe."

Jimmie Rocco pushed away from the table and quick as a bunny was out the door.

Pepper watched Jimmie leave. He stared at the door a long time before getting back to me.

"I learned some things about Domenic Light Fingers Conte," he said and then added, "more than I care to know. Conte was a punk from the Big Apple who specialized in five-finger discounts. Petty theft, breaking, and entering, those sorts of crimes. That's how he got his nickname of Light Fingers. Conti came to Chicago because he wanted to move into the narcotics traffic. Bad decision. But you already know that."

"I knew Conte tried muscling in on the narcotics trade. But I was second on his case," I said, "Eddie Fudge was the lead detective."

"It was Gerald Pascoe's territory that Conte had his eyes on," Pepper said. "Pascoe's business wasn't all Conte had eyes on. He wanted Maria Savona, Jerry Pascoe's girl."

"So, Jerry Pascoe doing away with Conte would make sense," I said. "We found Conte dead on his bed at the Lomax Hotel, and Maria Savona passed out on the bedroom floor, clutching the murder weapon, a thirty-eight revolver."

"What about Pascoe?" Pepper asked.

"He had an airtight alibi. He was playing poker with Terrance Johnson, his attorney. The men had a close relationship. Pascoe imagined himself as a respectable businessman. He owned a laundry mat and a gas station, but those stores were fronts for his narcotics trade. Pascoe was dirty as a sidewalk after a mudslide, but he was never busted. Johnson kept Pascoe out of jail on more than one occasion."

"And Johnson put Maria Savona in jail," Pepper said.

"How am I going to prove that Pascoe and not Maria Savona killed Domenic Conte? Gerald Pascoe died two years ago."

Pepper sighed. "That, my friend, I can't help you with."

"How did you find all of this out?" I asked.

"I have my sources," Pepper answered smugly. "As for Tony Conte, he still lives with Mom. They have a bungalow on Bridgeport. Pepper slid a slip of paper across the table.

"The address," he said.

CHAPTER 20

I rode the L back to the LaSalle Street station, where I grabbed a taxi. Finding a cab was easy. Paying for it was hard. The drive from LaSalle Street back to my place set me back. Cash was quickly burning a hole in my pocket. I decided the time was right to brush the dust off my Cadillac and do my own driving.

Before Chicago's winter's furry rolled into town, I stored the car in the garage behind my building. Like a hibernating bear, the car roared out of its winter sleep. I backed out of the garage and drove to the end of the alley, where I turned right on Lexington. A block down, I made a left turn onto 27th Avenue. I followed 27th Avenue to Bridgeport.

I stopped at the curb in front of the house. It was a two-story clapboard house with asphalt roof shingles built on narrow but long lot. The kind of house every town built after World War II. The houses were built so close to each other the joke was that neighbors could reach out from their bathroom windows and shake hands.

I double-checked the address with the paper Pepper had given me. It was the house Domenic Conte purchased for his mother when he moved her here from New York.

The house looked unkempt. Many of the asphalt roof tiles were missing having blown off during storms. Black roofing paper patched the holes. The paint around window trims and the front door had grown yellowed with age. Brown overgrown grass-like tumbleweeds swarmed over the front yard.

I got out of the car and walked up the cracked concrete sidewalk to the front door. A cheap wood screen door hung loosely against the entrance door. I pulled the screen door aside to knock on the front door.

Moments later, I heard tired footsteps shuffle to the door. A deadbolt clanked when unlocked, and the door squeaked opened. A rusted security chain stopped the door from opening wider. The round eye belonging to a black woman peeked through the separation between door jam and door

"You want something?" she asked.

"Does Mrs. Conti live here?" I asked. "Theresa Conti."

"Are you from the Welfare Department?"

"No, I'm a private detective," I said. I pushed my business card into her fingers.

To her, private detective sounded as bad as welfare official. She moved to slam the door, but I put my hand out and stopped it from closing.

"I don't mean to be rude," I said, "but who are you?"

"I'm Mrs. Conte's caregiver. Mrs. Conti is upstairs napping and can't come to the door."

"Maybe I could ask you one or two questions," I said.

The door slackened as the chain was released. The caretaker emerged from the doorway. She was portly in figure, wore an oversized green dress with a white collar. She held out her hands to block the sunlight from her eyes. Her hands were big, callused, and strong. Her face was just as big and strong.

"What do you want to know?" she asked.

"I only want to know about Tony," I said. "I'm not here about welfare or anything else."

The lady spat out the doorway.

"I gots no love lost for that boy," she said. "What's he done now?"

"Nothing," I said. "I only want to ask him about a man he might know."

"Boy only hangs out with junkies," she said. "He's not here. Only comes around to steal his mama's welfare checks."

"Do you know where he goes when he isn't here?" I asked.

"I told you the boy hangs out with junkies."

She reached around the backside of the door.

"These matchbooks are all over his bedroom." She handed me a matchbook.

"Alexandria's Hideaway? Is this where Tony hangs out?" I asked.

She nodded her head. "And doing who knows what with who. I got no use for that boy."

She spits out the doorway again and then slammed the door.

CHAPTER 21

I was parked across the street from Alexandria's Hideaway when a police car with lights flashing and siren screaming fishtailed to a stop in front of the place. Two cops jumped out and ran inside the club. The nightclub is a haven for drug dealers and buyers, so the arrival of a police car wasn't out of place. But when an ambulance and two more squads followed, and one belonging to Lieutenant Shakespeare made an appearance, that made me think that this wasn't normal.

I squeezed through the crowd of gathering onlookers to get to the front of the line. I held my badge up to the cop who guarded the door.

"That's a Peeper's shield," he said. "Only real cops are allowed inside." And he dismissed me with a wave of his hand.

Shakespeare, standing in the doorway, spotted me. He walked forward, placed a hand on the cop's shoulder, and whispered in his ear. The officer nodded. He then walked around us to deal with the growing crowd of rubberneckers.

"Somewhere in the back of my mind, I knew you would be here," Shakespeare said to me. "But, I half expected to see you lying on the floor covered in blood."

"Who is it?" I asked.

"Tony Conte," he said.

"Is he dead?" I asked.

"No, but close enough that I got the call. I guess the prognosis is he'll soon be heading that way. Do me a favor, Caruso. If you ever think that anything wrong is about to happen to me, keep it to yourself. I don't believe in coincidences, but this comes awful close. Not many hours ago we talked about Tony Conte, and low and behold there he is knocking on Heaven's door.

"I want to talk to him," I said.

"Sure. Why not. But you better hurry."

I walked inside Alexandria's. Music blared from loudspeakers suspended from the ceiling. Colored lights washed the walls in hues of sapphire and rose.

Tony Conte was laying on his back in the middle of the dance floor. A circle of red stained his shirt over his stomach. Blood dripped from his nose and mouth staining his teeth. Paramedics worked to save Tony's life, but I could tell that their efforts were naught by the glances they shared.

I knelt beside Tony. "Who did this to you, Tony?" I said.

His lips moved mouthing inaudible words. I leaned in closer to hear his last breath.

Shakespeare took a Diamond match from his pocket and struck it on the sole of one of the dead man's shoes. He lit his cigar, blew out the match, and tossed it aside. "I told you he was close to becoming 10-7," he said. "What did you hope to get out of him?"

I straightened up. "I don't know," I said. "Maybe something I could build on."

"Maybe you'll do better with the glee club," Shakespeare said, pointing to the line up of Alexandria's unusual clientele. "Although I wouldn't get my hopes up too high. This bunch hates cops. Vice and narcotics detectives routinely raid the club. One sideways look at those cops gets a guaranteed beating and ride to jail. Keeping their mouths shut and eyes to the floor are club rules. They post a list of what not to say to cops on the bathroom walls."

Shakespeare walked down the line inspecting each one like an Army sergeant looking over new recruits. The group was a diverse population of low-life scum. Men dressed in leather with long hair contrasted the women with their hair cut short wearing plaid shirts and jeans. Thin or fat, short or tall, black or white, and young or old, it didn't matter who they were because the one thing they had in common was they all hated cops.

A middle-aged man, thin and of average height, stepped forward. His dark hair was combed back off his forehead in a pompadour. His pants were tight leather, and he wore a floppy tank top. He claimed to be the elected spokesman for the group.

"Democracy in action," I said.

Shakespeare bit on his cigar. "I guess he thinks dressing that way makes him look young."

"Someone should tell him the effect isn't working," I said.

The man's name was Duster. I didn't question him on why.

"Tony was sitting at the bar minding his own business," Duster said.

"You knew Tony Conti?" Shakespeare said.

"Sure, everyone knew Tony."

"So tell me, how did Tony go from sitting at the bar minding his own business to laying dead on the floor?" I asked.

"Some guy came in and sat next to Tony."

"They knew each other?" Shakespeare asked.

Duster shrugged. "No, I don't think they did. At any rate, the guy wasn't a regular. I never saw him before, and no one here knew him."

"Okay, Tony minds his own business having a drink, and what happens next?" I said.

"Tony and this guy get into an argument. Tony tried to get up to move away, but the man pushed him back down on the stool. The gunshot was the next thing I heard, and I saw Tony fall to the floor. That's all I saw. I ran into the bathroom."

"I saw what happened," said a young black woman. She sat side-saddle on a bar stool, sipping a Brandy Alexander. "This place gets so fucking boring. I don't know why I come here. So when the excitement started, I sat back and watched the show."

She pulled a cigarette out of a pack resting in front of her on the bar and hung the smoke from her lips. I struck a match, and she took my hand to lift the match to her cigarette. The match brightened her face. I saw a mildly attractive face hidden under too much makeup. A bit of soap and water would clean her up to look good. She puckered her lips and blew out the match.

"No one stopped the guy," she said. "He shot poor Tony and just walked away."

I showed her the picture of Julio Silva.

"No, that's not the guy. That guy has a face like a mug. The guy who shot Tony looked like a cop."

"What do you mean, he looked like a cop?"

"He just did," she said. "Cops got a look. Not you. You're too pretty to be a cop. The shooter looked more like him." She pointed at Shakespeare.

She smiled at me. It was one of those smiles coming from a dame that I didn't mind seeing. But then she did this. She leaned into the woman next to her and kissed her on the lips.

"What a screwed up world we live in," she said. "You just wait and see what happens when we women take over. This world is going to change."

"I can hardly wait," I said, and I walked away.

CHAPTER 22

Shakespeare was waiting outside near his car. I joined him for a cigarette.

"Why would anyone want to kill Tony Conti?" Shakespeare asked. "The kid was a junkie with nothing to lose and nothing to gain."

I took a couple of drags off the Chesterfield and flipped it to the gutter. More and more every day, the nicotine rush wasn't doing it for me. I hoped that wasn't a sign of getting old.

"Don't you get it, Shakespeare?" I said. "Conti, Steele, Pascoe, Julio Silva, Maria Savona, the lawyers Pendleton, Johnson, and Ore they're all linked together like a Daisy

Chain. Like a string of dominoes, push one down, and they all fall."

"The witness said the shooter looked like a cop," Shakespeare said.

"Would it be anyone in your squad?" I said.

Shakespeare frowned. "My men are rough around the edges, but no one is a cold-blooded killer. I'll go back inside and get written statements from those two witnesses. Get them to come and sit with an artist. Maybe we can get a look at this guy."

Shakespeare huffed and flicked an ash off his cigar on his walk back to the nightclub. I pushed my way through the onlookers to my car.

When I got back to the office, a courier envelope waited for me. The return address said Northern Life and Trust Insurance Company. I tore open the flap and pulled out the copy of the life insurance policy on Phyllis Steele. The face value of the policy was half a million dollars. The beneficiary was Edward Steele.

I picked up the phone and dialed Katrina at her desk.

"I got the insurance policy you ordered," I told her.

"Is it an interesting read?" she asked.

"So far, so good, but I must be fair in my critique. I haven't gotten past the half of million dollars."

"That's a lot of money."

"Some people are worth more dead than they are alive," I said.

"Anyone, you know, come to mind?" she said.

I pushed the policy back into the envelope. "I'll bring this over to you as soon as I can. You do have good friends, Kitten. Obtaining a copy of an insurance policy isn't easy."

Katrina blew me an air kiss ending our conversation. No sooner than I hung up with Katrina did the telephone ring. I picked it up.

"Hello, Miss Pendleton," I said.

"How did you know it was me?" she asked.

"I'm clairvoyant as well as charming," I said.

"I was planning on being clandestine," she said.

"I'm a detective, Miss Pendleton. I'm trained to notice."

"Call me, Amelia."

"Only if you call me Joe."

"I'd like that."

"Now that we have dispensed with formality, what do I owe the pleasure of this phone call?"

"I thought we could meet."

"Professionally or socially?"

"Professionally at first. We'll see what happens after that."

"You're secretive again."

"See you at seven in the Oasis Lounge inside the Donnelly Hotel."

"The Donnelly is a dive. Surely, you can do better."

"I'll be waiting in the back booth."

She hung up, leaving me trying to squeeze one last syllable out of the phone. Amelia Pendleton had the sweetest voice that curled my toes. No matter how much I heard, I wanted to hear more.

I folded the insurance form into my pocket and checked my wristwatch. It was a quarter after six — no time to go by the newsroom. I put on my hat and left for my meeting with Amelia Pendleton.

CHAPTER 23

Amelia Pendleton looked out of place sitting in the Oasis Lounge. The Donnelly Hotel isn't the Ritz Carlton, and the Oasis Lounge isn't the Pump Room. She stuck out like a silver coin in a penny-ante game of craps.

The lighting in the barroom cast dimly over the interior, undoubtedly intentional, so no one noticed the worn furnishing. The air smelled the kind of sour that used cigarette smoke, cheap whiskey, and bad breath brings. I walked over to the back booth where Amelia waited, and I sat.

"I ordered you a gin martini," Amelia said. "Dry and dirty. I thought that was how you liked it."

I picked up on her dry and dirty metaphor winked at her as I took up the goblet and sipped the drink. It was dry the way I liked a martini with barely a splash of vermouth. Sir Winston Churchill, a notorious martini connoisseur, insisted that the bottle of vermouth stay corked and across the room when making his favorite drink. A dash of olive juice mixed in with the gin gave the martini a dirty sour zing.

"Did you know the invention of the modern-day police force came into being because of Londoners drinking too much gin?" I said. I sipped again.

Amelia raised her glass. "Then we have the Brits to thank for getting drunk," she said.

I laughed. "Sister, you have all the cute answers. Maybe you can get a job as the duck on Groucho's television show You Bet Your Life."

She rolled an olive around the glass with the pick, then stabbed it and showing off a certain sensuality plucked the green fruit into her mouth.

"Shall we get business out of the way?" she asked.

"All work and no play makes Joe a boring boy," I said.

She smiled. "I understand. However, I have a job to do."

I was beginning to think that I might be getting set up for a tumble.

"My boss, Mr. Steele, understands your obligation to finalize the job his wife paid you to do. Like you, he, too, is a businessman. He respects promises made are promises kept. But your contract ended with Mrs. Steele's death. Mr. Steele relieves you of any further obligation in finding Julio Silva. In return, he has thought to pay you for your services generously."

Amelia pushed the envelope across the table.

"This is yours," she said.

I took the envelope, unsealed it, and thumbed through the bills inside.

"There's more money here than I did work for," I said.

"Mr. Steele's way of saying thank you."

"Or is it Mr. Steele's way of saying back off?"

Amelia's lily-white face showed the slightest purge of red.

"You're not going to be impolite and spoil our afternoon, are you, Joe?"

"Call me nuts. God knows I can use the money. But behind this handsome, charming exterior is an old fashion dye in the wool conservative boy who believes in working for the things I need. Sometimes I come by those things the hard way because I don't except free rides, bribes, or easy money. I still get by. So, you can tell your boss no deal." I closed the envelope and dropped it on the table in front of Amelia. "This case is over when I say it's over."

Amelia picked up her glass, tilted her head back, and drank the rest of her martini.

"You should take the money, Joe. Forget you ever heard the name, Julio Silva. Get away for a time. Take a vacation."

She could have knocked me off my chair, saying those things. If deja vu wasn't anything more than a hippie catchword, then I was reliving my history.

I said, "Another person with another envelope full of money gave me that same advice. He, too, said I should take a vacation. Go to Florida, he told me. I don't like Florida. I sunburn easily, I don't play golf or tennis, and I hate mosquitos, bugs, and snakes. I didn't take his advice like I'm not taking yours."

"You're unreasonable, Joe. Please, accept this money and stop looking for Julio Siva."

"That sounds like a plea."

"You like me, don't you, Joe?"

"You have a certain enchanting quality that I find irresistible. But if you're the pawn sent to checkmate the king, then my answer is no."

She pouted her lower lip. "You're rude."

"If you think that was rude, get a load of this. I'm beginning to think that Edward Steele killed his wife?"

I produced the insurance policy and slapped it down on the table.

"That's a life insurance policy worth half of a million dollars Steele took out on his wife."

Amelia laughed. "Edward killed Phyllis for life insurance money. How garden variety. I was hoping you could do better than that, Joe."

"No, not for the insurance money. Although it does make for a nice accompaniment, I think the reason Edward Steele killed his wife dates back a few years. Dates back to Jerry Pascoe, Maria Savona, and Julio Silva."

Amelia tensed frigid like a sculpture. "Have you shared your suspicions with the police?"

"Not yet," I said.

"Who else has seen the insurance policy?"

"Only me."

"Not your reporter, girlfriend."

"Katrina ordered the copy, but she hasn't seen it."

"You should keep it that way," she said. Her demeanor changed back to the sensual playmate. "We can still enjoy the afternoon together. All you have to do is put the envelope in your pocket and agree to stop looking for Julio Silva."

"Oh, I have stopped looking for Silva. He found me. You might say that Julio Silva is my client. He paid me to prove that his sister Maria is innocent of the murder of Domenic Conte.

Julio claims Jerry Pascoe killed Conte in a jealous rage. Jerry Pascoe's lawyer, Terrance Johnson, got Pascoe off the hook and set up Maria Savona. Hey, wasn't Jerry Pascoe and your boss, Edward Steele, in business together. Didn't they manage Julio Silva's boxing career? Oh, I see by the frown on your face that I hit a sensitive nerve. Well, you're going to have a panic attach hearing this. Isn't Terrance Johnson one of your brother's law partners?"

Amelia Pendleton, all five foot seven of her majestic body, stood up. "You are making a big mistake, Mr. Caruso."

"So now it's Mr. Caruso. No, Joe, let's be friends?"

If looks could kill, I'd be laying on a slab in the county morgue right now. Amelia swirled, knocking over my martini in the process of leaving the Oasis Lounge in a huff.

CHAPTER 24

I caught up to Katrina at the Billy Goat Tavern. She was sitting at the bar with two reporters from the Tribune. I ordered a double bourbon, and she and I carried our drinks to a table in the back of the room. I gave her Steele's life insurance policy and told her about my meeting with Amelia Pendleton.

"She tried buying you off the case?" Katrina asked.

"Someone did. Amelia was the messenger."

"Amelia? You're on a first-name basis with her?"

"Strictly business. Anyway, we didn't leave that way. She became upset after I tied her brother and his law partners to Steele, Silva, and Savona."

"Down south, that arrangement is called a good ole boy club," Katrina said.

I said: "In Chicago, it's called business as usual."

"Speaking of Edward Steele," Katrina said. "I dug into his finances. He's in debt up to his eyebrows. Redeeming his wife's $500,000 life insurance policy would make that debt go away and still have leftovers."

"Phyllis' murder suspect shifts away from Julio Silva to Edward Steele?" I said.

"After your talk with Julio, you had a feeling that he might not have killed her," Katrina said.

I finished my drink and waved over a waitress for another. "He loved Phyllis," I said to Katrina. "Sure, he was sore at her for jilting him, but killing her didn't make sense. But Edward Steele? Granted, he's a big man who could inflict physical damage. Maybe he slaps her around from time to time, but I don't see him beating his wife to death."

"Was battery the official cause of her death?"

My drink came, and I took a sip. "I can't answer that," I said.

"What was the medical examiner's report from her autopsy?"

I shook my head. "Come to think of it; I don't know.

"Shakespeare would know," said Katrina.

"Let's have a bite to eat here before going to see him. Shakespeare is always eating, and he'll never share."

We ordered cheeseburgers and beers. While we ate, we didn't talk about corporal punishment and crime. Sports always came in first with me. Spring training kicked off, and opening day at Wrigley was fast approaching. Katrina's focus was on fashion and entertainment. A new play, American

Buffalo, opens next week at the Goodman Theatre that she wanted to see. I'm not a Broadway buff, but Katrina assured me that I would like the production, so I said I would go.

We wrapped up our diner and decided to by-pass talking to Shakespeare and drove to the medical examiner's office to speak with Doctor Peterson.

Peterson was standing next to her desk when we came in. She was wearing a long dress and a white blouse. The first time I saw her, she wore her hair in a bun that drew her facial muscles back, which made her look angry. Her hair was down, and her face relaxed. She still looked like she sucked on a few lemons before we came in.

"Come with me," Peterson said.

We followed her into a room off to the side of her office, which was a smaller room with medical devices. I didn't begin to recognize their use. Peterson pulled an x-ray film from a drawer and affixed it to a light table.

"I ruled the deceased woman's death a homicide caused by blunt force trauma." She switched on the light table. The x-ray illuminated so we could see a scan of Phyllis Steele's skull. Peterson pointed at a darken mark on the side of the skull. "This woman was struck from behind with an object that I believe was a hammer."

"And that caused her death?" Katrina asked.

Peterson looked skeptically at Katrina. "Of course," she said flatly. "Can you see these stress marks on the skull?" She pointed out the lines running down the skull from the area of impact. "Her skull nearly split in two. I also removed pieces of bone lodged in the brain tissue, and severe bleeding of the brain took place. No one survives that."

"And what about the beating to her body?" I asked.

"Post mortem," Peterson said. "The beating occurred after the fatal blow to her head."

Doctor Peterson switched off the light table and returned the x-ray to its drawer. We followed her back into her office.

"I released the body to the family," Peterson said.

"That was fast," I said. "Does Lieutenant Shakespeare know?"

"Yes. I phone the Lieutenant. He wasn't happy with me, but there wasn't a thing I could do to prevent the removal. The husband's attorney had all of the proper paperwork."

"Pendleton," I said to Katrina.

"You did take fingerprints and a blood sample?" I asked Peterson.

"No. I was bared by a court order."

"Isn't that unusual?" Katrina asked.

"Yes, in normal cases, but the attorney obtained the signature of a former judge."

"Jacob Pendleton," Katrina said.

"People from a funeral home accompanied the attorney," Peterson said. "They took the remains straight away to a crematorium. I suspect that Mrs. Phyllis Steele is a pile of ash by now."

CHAPTER 25

The doorman at Edward Steele's apartment building recognized me from my first visit. He winked at Katrina and let us inside without so much as a hello. The elevator carried us to the penthouse floor. Amelia Pendleton answered the door.

"You cannot be here," she said, guarding the doorway.

"I need to see your boss," I said.

I could have said more if given a chance, but before I could get another word out, Amelia started to close the door. I leaned my shoulder into the door to push my way into the apartment.

Amelia sprung on me like a panther on a rabbit. I couldn't get set fast enough to hold off her assault. Before I could take a breath, she had my arm wrapped around my back and her arm lassoing my neck. She was quick and strong for a woman. She pushed me out of the apartment.

"What's the commotion? Edward Steele asked, coming out from whatever room he hide inside.

"It's Caruso," Amelia said to him. She still held me in a bear hug.

All the while, Katrina was taking this in with a great deal of amusement.

Let him go, Amelia," Steele ordered.

She loosened her grip, and I slid out of her embrace. I pulled on my necktie, giving my neck muscles room to heal.

"Give him a drink," he said to Amelia. "I'll see him in the sitting room. Alone. The reporter stays in the hallway."

"Wait one cotton picking minute," Katrina said, in protest.

"Nothing against you personally, Miss Warring, but I don't want to see my name in print tomorrow."

I shrugged at Katrina just as Amelia yanked me back inside."

"I'm leaving," Katrina yelled to me.

Steele disappeared to another room as Amelia slammed the door. She then pushed me toward the back of the penthouse to the kitchen.

The kitchen was big, modern, and bright with loads of stainless steel. The appliances seemed top of the line stuff, but I wouldn't know my kitchen looks like a dump.

Amelia went to the sink, filled a glass with tap water, and handed it to me.

"He told you to give me a drink," I said.

She nudged the glass closer. "This is a drink."

I twitched my nose. "That's water. You shower with water. Cook pasta in water. You don't drink it."

She put the glass down in the sink. "What would you rather have?"

"Bourbon."

"Do you have a specific brand?" she asked, sarcastically.

I smiled. "The most expensive bourbon Steele has," I said.

She opened an upper cabinet and pulled out a bottle with four roses on the label. I nodded my approval, and she poured. When she stopped, I pressured her hand to pour more.

"I'm thirsty," I said.

Amelia smirked and filled the glass. "Come," she said. "Mr. Steele hates waiting."

"You're holding a grudge," I said, following her out of the kitchen.

"A grudge about what?" she said, walking.

"You left the Oasis Lounge abruptly. I thought you and I hit it off."

She stopped and turned. "You are shameful. I would rather hit it off with a goat."

I shrugged. "So, there is hope for us yet," I said.

She huffed, spun on her heels, and walked ahead. At the end of the hallway, she told me to go inside the room. I opened the door to a cozy room with thick curtains over the windows, Tiffany lamps on antique side tables, and a sofa that looked too comfortable to sit on.

Edward Steele sat in a chair with his legs crossed. He held a cigar between the fingers of his left hand and a glass in his right hand. Cigar smoke curled up to the ceiling disappearing in a white cloud. The ice in the highball glass tinkled when Steele's thumped his index finger against the glass.

"Sit down, Caruso," Steele said.

I only met Edward Steele once before, but I learned as much about him during that visit than I cared to know. Steele was a decisive man use to getting his way. Those below his social and economic structure, he treated with disrespect. Those above, I suspect, he envied and emulated. I fell in the first category. I could read his dislike for me in his body language. Sitting straight-backed with crossed legs told me to keep my distance. His finger drumming against the cocktail glass showed me his annoyance with my being there. And how he looked at me with lowered eyebrows signaled his negative feeling toward me.

And I'm such a lovable guy.

I sat down across from him.

"You cremated your wife's body?" I said.

"Yes," he said.

"Without a memorial service and funeral."

"I don't believe in either. They only prolong the grieving."

"And you like to get on with life as soon as possible. Is that it?"

"Something like that. Now, can I ask you a question?"

"Absolutely."

Steele stood to go to a cart with bottles on it to refresh his drink. He returned to his chair and sat back down in it.

"Why did you refuse my payment?" he asked.

"It felt more like a pay off than a payment," I said.

Steele placed his glass on the table and his cigar in an ashtray. He leaned forward.

"What's your game, Caruso?"

I sipped leisurely on the bourbon. I rested the glass on my knee before answering. I wanted Steele to feel restless while he awaited my response.

"Explain the life insurance policy you took out on your wife," I said.

"You know about that?"

I nodded.

"So, what about it? Everyone has a policy."

"Not for a half a million bucks."

Steele leaned back. "The policy was Phil's idea," he said.

"And who's idea was it to kill your wife?"

"Julio Silva killed Phyllis. You know that."

"Your wife was hit on the head from behind with a hammer. And then her killer beat her to make it look like Silva."

"You're wrong. Silva killed Phyllis."

"Silva didn't kill your wife. He loved her."

Steele stood and went to the door and opened it.

"I've heard enough," he said. "It's time that you left."

"You're having money problems, Steele, that $500,00 would cure."

"Leave."

"You made certain that your wife's body wasn't blood sampled or fingerprinted. You had her remains cremated to destroy evidence."

Steele's composure broke. His face reddened, and his fists clenched at his sides.

"Leave now, Caruso, or I'll physically throw you out."

I finished my drink, got up, and walked to the door.

"Sure, I'll leave, but I'll be back, and you can rest on that. Funny, isn't it Steele? That it's your time that is running out now."

CHAPTER 26

Katrina had gone back to work. I considered going there to tell her what had gone down between Edward Steele and me, but on second thought decided to go home. My duel with Steele left me hungry and thirsty. I had a pastrami sandwich and a cold bottle of beer waiting for me in my refrigerator.

I had a visitor in my apartment.

He didn't hear me walk up behind him bent at the waist with his head inside my refrigerator. His right hand was resting on the top of the refrigerator door as a balance while he searched inside my Frigidaire.

"If you're looking for a bottle of beer, it's on the bottom shelve of the door," I said.

The man pulled himself out, holding my pastrami sandwich tight in his left hand. My mustard dotted his lips.

He stood slightly shorter than me when he straightened up. His body grew thicker from his chest to his waist. He let out a deep breath that pushed his gut out beyond the waistband of his trousers and stretched the buttons of his jacket uncomfortably long to their corresponding holes.

"Good sandwich?" I said.

He swallowed. "Very good. Where did you get it?"

"Sammie's Deli," I said. "Leave a buck fifty on the table when you leave."

He looked at the sandwich and then at me. "It's a good sandwich, but not buck fifty good."

"Where can you find a better sandwich for that price?"

"In Philly," he said. He took another bite.

"You're from Philadelphia?" I said.

"Sometimes," he answered, chewing with his mouth open.

"Who are you?" I asked.

"I've been known by a name or two," he said.

"Which name are you going by tonight?"

He scratched his head with his free right hand. "Smith. Or is it Wesson? I get confused some days."

"Smith and Wesson. Okay, fella, I get the joke. What are you doing here?"

"There's no joke, Peeper," he said.

He produced a Smith and Wesson revolver from his jacket pocket, aimed it at me, and pulled the trigger.

CHAPTER 27

The nurse at the hospital kept telling me how lucky I was to be alive. "Two inches to your right and the bullet would have entered your heart. Instead of resting on this cushy bed in a private room with me taking care of you, you would be lying on a hard slab in the mortuary."

So much for a cheerful bedside manner.

The doctor's bedside manner was much better. "The bullet entered the muscle of your right shoulder just below the collarbone, and exited the other side," he said. "In and out with no major damage. You should be out of here in a couple of days."

My interpretation of a couple of days means two days. I learned that in doctors speak a couple of days means anywhere from five to seven days.

Shakespeare came to see me three times. Duck Rizzo once, and like a good neighbor, brought my mail. All bills, so I threw them in the trash. Amelia Pendleton, surprise, surprise, stopped by. I figure she came by to see if I was on my deathbed. Since I wasn't, she didn't stay long. Katrina seldom left my side.

I checked out after day four. The food was too horrid to stay a day longer.

I went home, took a shower, and changed clothes. I treated myself to a cheeseburger and beer at Lou's Diner. Feeling as good as a man that missed death by two inches could feel I pressed my luck and took a taxi to the law office of Jacob Pendleton, Terrace Johnson, and Fredrick Ore.

"Are you out of your mind going there?" Katrina said, sitting beside me in the backseat of the taxi.

"Pendleton is the only one I haven't spoken to," I said. "It's about time I asked him a question or two."

"I don't think you'll get an answer from him."

"I have my ways," I said.

"Your ways are as tactful as a military interrogation," Katrina said. "These men make their livings working in and out of the written law. Your blitzkrieg tactics will never penetrate their thick skins. Beating them at their game is what will work best. The power of the press is a dangerous tool to use against bullies like these men. That's why I should do the talking, and you should, well, keep quiet.

She made a good argument. Tact has never been my strong suit. I agreed to keep a civil profile and speak when spoken to.

The taxi let us out in front of 611 LaSalle Street. Compared to the taller buildings around it, the twelve-story structure was modest in size. The elevator zoomed us up to the tenth floor. Katrina checked in with the receptionist.

"Mr. Pendleton's schedule is full today," the receptionist said. She was an older woman conservatively dressed wearing a lady's business suit that added to her maternal appearance.

Katrina produced her press credentials and explained the purpose of her being there. "To question Mr. Pendleton about the death of Phyllis Steele."

"And you?" she asked me, peering above the rim of pearl frame eyeglasses. "Are you also from the press?"

I nodded, honoring my pledge to Katrina of keeping shut my mouth.

The receptionist gave us one new look before picking up the receiver. Placing it to her ear and mouth, she punched two numbers on the switchboard. I presumed the call connected her to Jacob Pendleton. The receptionist spoke discreetly into the mouthpiece. Falling silent to listen, she nodded. Returning the receiver to its cradle, she pointed to the waiting room and chairs.

"Sit and wait," she instructed. "Mr. Pendleton will be with you when he can."

Given no opportunity for rebuttal, we obliged and retreated to the waiting room. Sunshine streamed through the large clear glass windows washing the room in light and raising the temperature a degree above uncomfortable. I sat and watched the minute hand of a wall clock move with the speed of a turtle while Katrina busied herself reading old magazines. The lobby served as the hub with a variety of rooms and offices connected to it. Forty-five minutes passed as did an endless procession of suited men coming and leaving those rooms and offices. The disorderly half of me wanted to storm the receptionist to object to our waiting period. But I didn't. Slamming my hand down on her desk and barking off a few choice words might make the receptionist blush, but it would not get Katrina and me into the private office of Jacob Pendleton any sooner. So, I sat quietly and waited.

Finally, the office door opened, and to my surprise out walked Amelia Pendleton.

"My brother will see you now," Amelia said. Her invitation aimed at me, not Katrina.

Katrina jumped to her feet. Katrina is short. Wearing heels, she's maybe five foot five. Amelia Pendleton towered over her.

"Wait one minute," Katrina said, not giving up any ground to the taller woman. "You kept me away from interviewing Steele, and now you're attempting to do the same with your brother. I won't stand for it. The Daily News won't stand for it."

"My brother has business to discuss with Mr. Caruso," Amelia said.

"I'm coming in. Just try to stop me," Katrina said.

Amelia surrendered. "Suit yourself."

Jacob Pendleton was a short man with a round face and soft jowls like a chipmunk's stocked with acorns. White, like flecks of snowflakes sprinkled throughout his unruly dark hair. His nose protruded out to a point from between a set of squinty eyes. He sat behind a desk that looked two sizes too big for a person of his height.

Amelia walked around to her brother's side of the desk to whisper in his ear. Both sets of eyes were firmly in place on Katrina. His sister's conversation concluded when Jacob nodded, waving her off. Amelia came around to the front of the desk, finding a chair beside me to sit on.

"Please, take seats, Mr. Caruso and Miss Warring," Jacob Pendleton said, using his most authoritarian lawyer voice. "I expected to see you sooner, Mr. Caruso. What took you so long getting here?"

"I took a detour at a hospital to recover from a gunshot wound," I said.

"I'm sorry to hear that," Pendleton said, looking smug like a cat that just ate a canary. "The business you're in can be dangerous. No doubt, you keep an eye out over your shoulder."

"I do time and again," I said. "But I'd much rather keep my eyes focused ahead."

Katrina took a step forward, bridging the air gap between her and Pendleton's desk. "I would like to ask you some questions," she said.

The lawyer gestured open-handed to the chairs in front of his desk. "My office, Miss. Warring, my questions," he said. Accustomed to getting his way notwithstanding, he repeated his invitation to sit with authority. "Now, sit down."

Katrina and I sat.

Jacob Pendleton held high a sheet of paper waving it as if he were auditioning for the Royal Navy Signal Corp. "I believe you know what a cease and desist order is, Mr. Caruso," he said. "But if you have forgotten the rules of law, I'll refresh your memory. A cease and desist order directs a person to stop doing something immediately. That is every man's definition, but I can go into more legal aspects if you prefer?"

"I know what a C & D is," I said.

"My client is Edward Steele. Mr. Steele wants you to stop bothering him. He wishes that you stop immediately."

"That is ridiculous," I said.

"That is your opinion. My client believes that you pose a problem to his security and wellbeing. Stay away from Edward Steele, Mr. Caruso."

"Your sister attempted to bribe me," I said.

Jacob Pendleton turned to his sister. His eyes opened wide in question.

"I did not," Amelia said.

"She's lying," I said. "Last week, we met at the Donnelly Hotel in the Oasis Lounge."

"Amelia tossed her hair back. "I would never go inside the Donnelly Hotel," she said.

"She handed me an envelope containing a large sum of money. The money was hush money. I guess that was her idea of a cease and desist order."

"I have no idea what you're referring to," Pendleton said. He turned to see Katrina holdinh ger small recorder. "What are you recording?" he asked.

"Notes for my story," she said.

"Stop immediately."

"You can't make me. Freedom of the press, remember?"

Jacob Pendleton stood up. "We're done," he said.

"What was Edward Steele's business relationship with Jerry Pascoe," Katrina asked.

"I don't have to answer that," Pendleton said.

"How about Mrs. Steele and Julio Silva?"

"I'm not answering that question either. Are you done, Miss Warring?"

"No, I'm just getting started. Some years ago, a young woman, Maria Savona, was her name, was prisoned for the murder of Domenic Conte, a known gangster. My source tells me that she is innocent of that crime. Jerry Pascoe killed Conte. Considering Edward Steele's close ties to Jerry Pascoe, would Mr. Steele have had anything to do with that murder?"

Pendleton stomped to the door. Get out," he said, pointing. "And Caruso take the cease and desist order with you on your way."

I picked up the paper from his desk, crumpled it, and threw it at Pendleton.

"Be very careful, Mr. Caruso," Pendleton said. "You will wind up in jail if you do anything as foolish as disobeying that order."

"I've been in jail before," I said. "And now that you mentioned going to jail. What do you know about my being shot?"

Pendleton pointed to the open door. "Get out," he said.

CHAPTER 28

"That went well," Katrina said, sarcastically. "You got a cease and desist order, and I got nothing."

"Some people have all the fun," I said.

The traffic light on the corner of LaSalle and Dearborn Streets changed from red to green, and we walked quickly across LaSalle. An English Pub on the corner where paralegals go after work to sip martinis and talk about their caseloads looked inviting. We went in for drinks.

The British flags roped together hanging from the ceiling were the first things we noticed. Then there was the picture of her majesty Queen Elizabeth. From her royal birth over the bar, she watched the crowd of merrymakers thick with lively talk and robust laughter. It was all reminiscent of scenery from an old spy movie. I could almost smell the Swiss eggs in the kitchen and taste the black and tan ale.

We sat at a table next to a window and ordered gin and tonic cocktails. While we waited for our drinks, we watched the parade of three-piece suited men, and conservative dressed ladies stroll up and down LaSalle Street.

"I could have easily had a job like they have," Katrina said, reminiscing her past.

"Working nine to five and wearing an appropriate dress," I said.

"And having a chauvinist pig for a boss," she said, with gayety.

We nodded our thanks to the waitress who dropped off our drinks.

I held up my glass in a toast. "Instead, you chose the exciting career of crime reporting."

Katrina clinked my glass with hers. "And I have you to thank for that," she said.

We drank and watched the crowd some more.

"Was it Pendleton who tried paying you off?" Katrina asked.

"Either him or Steele. Perhaps both."

"Do you think Pendleton arranged to have someone shoot you?" Katrina said.

"I got shot after I turned down the money. Pendleton is as good a suspect as anyone."

We stayed quiet, watching more of the passing parade. Katrina poked at the ice cubes in her glass with a swizzle stick. The ice cubes made a tinkling sound bouncing off the glass and sliding into each other. With a faraway look, Katrina watched.

"Where are we going from here, Joe?" she asked softly. She lifted her head. Tears started to cloud her green eyes. "I don't mean today. Where are we going tomorrow, next month, next year? What's our future, Joe?"

I took her hand. "This comes up every time we work together on a dangerous case, Kitten. The answer is always the same. One day at a time. With the kind of jobs we have there isn't any other way."

"We could change all of that."

"You tried that, don't you remember? After the Arthur Mitchell case, you ran off to California looking for a different life."

"Bringing that up is not fair, Joe. We came within a heartbeat of getting killed. I was stressed and couldn't sleep nights or work during the day. I had to get away."

"You stayed in California for six months. And what happened?"

"I came back."

"Before California, it was Europe and before that, New York. You came back every time. Your job and this city are what make you the person that you are. You love them too much to leave."

Katrina pulled my hand to her lips and kissed. "And I love you, Joe. I come back to you."

"And I'm happy that you do, Kitten. I love you too."

We held hands, and suddenly the crowded barroom became silent.

CHAPTER 29

The Beatles' song A Hard Days Night was playing over a pocket transistor radio. The multitrack voices of Lennon and McCartney sounded shrill coming from the miniature speaker. George Harrison's guitar riffs clattered, and Ringo's drums clashed with the melody like he was beating on the bottoms of pots and pans.

"I started to wonder if I'd ever see you again, Julio," I said.

Julio Silva stepped out from the shadow of an obese maple tree. Wetlands and vegetation surround the McKinley Park Lagoon. An unusual place for a meeting since the lagoon has a history for attracting undesirable activity at nightfall. I felt uneasy being there.

"I heard you got shot and laid up in a hospital," said Julio. "I thought I'd let you rest."

"How compassionate of you," I said.

"Maria is still in jail," he said.

"I told you that would take time."

"Maria don't have time."

"In the eyes of the law, Maria is guilty."

Julio stepped forward. If there were a moon out tonight, his body would drape a shadow over me. He slapped me open-handed across the face. That portion of my face felt warm as the damaged blood vessels rushed in blood.

"What was that for?" I asked.

"Maria is not guilty. You get her out of jail."

"I told you that wasn't going to be easy."

He slapped me again—this time on the other side of my face.

"I let the first one go," I said, rubbing my face. "I'll do the same for the second, but not if you hit me again. I don't give a damn how much taller you are than me or broader you are in the shoulders or that you once fought professionally. I'll fight back."

The lagoon steamed with humidity. Beads of sweat dripped from Julio's forehead. He unclenched his fists went to a picnic bench and sat. The radio in his pocket blared a Bob Dylan song. Something about a rolling stone.

"Do me a favor, Julio, and turn off the radio."

He looked up at me. His eyes were soft like a dog housed in a kennel. "I liked listening to music in the joint," he said.

"You don't like my music?"

"Music?"

"Oh, I get it. You're a chamber music guy."

"I don't know what chamber music is," I said. "Just turn the radio off so we can talk."

Julio reached a hand inside his coat pocket to turn off the radio. His hand came out holding a gun.

Just a few seconds ago, his eyes showed a softness, but now they changed to angry eyes.

"I paid you two hundred bucks to get Maria out of jail. You didn't do that."

"Put the hardware down, Julio," I said. "I need more time. Let me explain. I think that Phyllis Steele's death, you and your sister's circumstances are all connected. I just have to find the person pulling the strings."

"I loved Phil. I told you that."

"Sure, you loved her, but you never said that you didn't kill her."

"You starting that again?"

"Don't get your shoulders in a huff, big boy. The police still consider you suspect numero uno."

"You want me to confess? If confessing to killing Phil will get Maria out of jail, then I will."

"Put the gun down and let us talk this over," I said.

Julio pressed the barrel of the gun against my forehead.

"You got three more days," he said.

"I'll need more," I said. "How about a week?"

"Three days. If you ain't got anything, then I don't need you."

Julio backed away his heavy footsteps crushing leaves as he walked into the shadows of the lagoon.

I breathed a sigh of relief.

Out in the lagoon, a fish jumped, and an owl hooted.

I sat down on the picnic bench just long enough for my knees to stop shaking. I stood up and started for my car. I made myself a promise. If Julio Silva ever pulled a stunt like that on me again, I would kill him.

I got in my car and drove away.

CHAPTER 30

The hour was late, but I didn't care. I went back to the office. I took the office bottle from the deep desk drawer and poured a stiff drink. The first drink didn't do anything to calm my nerves. The second drink made everything look more transparent, and after the third drink, I didn't care.

I pulled on the top drawer where I keep my forty-five. Why I didn't pack it tonight was a mystery. I swore never to do that again.

The telephone rang. The sweet-sounding voice on the other end rescued me from feeling more remorse. She was calling from Mark Gorman. At first, I didn't place the man with the name. And then it hit me. Mark Gorman was Cheesy Gorman, a former confidential informant who sold lady's lingerie. Those sexy women's garments like push-up bras, and see-through panties that working girls wore in gentlemen clubs, and strip shows. Even the rich Gold Coast wives who wanted to keep their sugar daddy husbands happy bought that cheesy stuff from Gorman. Hence the nickname, Cheesy.

"Can you meet with Mr. Gorman say in one hour at his office?" the sweet, young voice asked.

I yawned. "Cheesy wants to meet at this hour?" I asked.

The voice chuckled. "Mr. Gorman doesn't sleep much. Is one hour, okay? Do you want the address?"

I didn't feel keen on going outside again tonight, but Gorman always has his ear to the ground. He has connections, so he must know something. Why else would he want to meet with me? I said yes to meeting Cheesy and no to needing the address.

Cheesy kept an office on the second floor of the Textile Discount Outlet Building on 21st Street in Chicago's garment district. A yellow bug light hung over the single door entrance. Mosquitoes and other tiny flying insects buzzed around the light knocking themselves silly. The door was unlocked, so I walked inside.

The warehouse was as wide inside as it was long. Colored fabrics of various weaves lay folded or spooled on tables and shelves. I walked to the rear of the warehouse, where a wooden staircase reached Cheesy's office.

The office was small, like Cheesy, and cluttered. Also, like Cheesy. He sat in a chair in front of his desk with his size eight feet up on the edge. Using a Tootsie Roll Pop sucker that he pulled out of his mouth, he motioned me to a chair next to him. I sat in it.

"What's it been, Caruso, three, four years?"

I could smell the booze coming off his breath. Cheesy liked drinking whiskey like most people liked drinking water. A bad liver didn't stop his boozing. Like warning a smoker that cigarettes kill, they go on puffing. Cheesy kept drinking.

I shouldn't talk. I'm guilty of both.

"I may have gotten older, packed on a few extra pounds since our last meet, and my hair is thinner, but my dick still gets stiff, and my hearing is good."

Cheesy always liked talking about himself first before getting around to talking about anyone else.

Cheesy brought his feet to the floor and leaned forward to get closer to me. "I hear you have an interest in Phyllis Steele," he said. "I hear your ankles are deep in shit, and you need shoveling out. Am I right, or am I wrong? What say you?"

I tilted my head to one side. "Who gave you that tad bit of information?" I asked.

"And why would I tell you that?"

"For old time's sake," I said.

Cheesy sucking on the Tootsie Roll Pop made a slurping noise. "I knew guys that did things for old time's sake," he said. "They never lived to see their old times. There has to be more in it for me to get involved."

I tilted my head to the other side. "I can be a good friend when trouble raises its ugly beak," I said.

Cheesy tilted his head. "Like how you helped that newspaper reporter girlfriend of yours almost getting killed? That good of a friend?"

My eyes drew to slits. I had a good mind to walk out, but I was curious about what Cheesy had to say, so I stayed and let that roll off me.

"I told you, I still hear things," Cheesy said. He removed the sucker from his mouth and pointed it at me. "Now lets us get serious. I'm willing to sell you my information for a price."

"Good old Cheesy," I said. I slumped in the chair to wait for the hit.

"I want into Roxy's Speakeasy," Cheesy said.

Roxanne Murphy owned Roxy's Speakeasy, a hi-classed strip joint on the north side of the city. Roxanne and I had a fling when Katrina went to live in California. That ended when Katrina came back. Despite my brush off, Roxy still considered me her friend.

"I want Roxy to buy my undies for her girls," Cheesy said. "And not only a couple of sets. I want a contract for a whole shit load."

"And what makes you think that I can pull that off?" I asked.

"I've been trying to break that broad for years with no luck. Since you once tapped her, you can be my ace in a hole. Pardon the pun. She buys my shit, and I tell you what I know."

"I'll need a down payment," I said. "Some collateral to get the ball rolling."

Cheesy shoved the Tootsie Roll Pop back into his mouth and sucked. "I've been trying to quit smoking," he said.

"And how is that going for you?" I asked.

"These help, but now I'm addicted to these little sugary treats."

"There's always something," I said.

Cheesy nodded. He sucked again. "Here's what I'll do," he said. "I'll give you the guy that tried bumping you off. He goes by the name Johnny Million. He's staying at a fleabag flophouse on the south side. The Donnelly Hotel. You know that place?"

"I do," I said. It was in the hotel's bar where I met with Amelia Pendleton. I didn't tell Cheesy that. Somehow, I thought he already knew.

"Million eats at the Noodle House around the corner. I'll give you more once you give me more. Deal?"

Cheesy struck out his. I didn't take it. His hand looked sticky."

"Deal," I said. And I stood up and left.

CHAPTER 31

I sat at the table where Amelia Pendleton and I sat in the Oasis Bar in the Donnelly Hotel. The bartender recognized me and brought over a glass of Old Granddad whiskey. I asked him about Johnny Million. The bartender was an older gent. He told me he was close to retiring and explained that he wanted to see that day. He hoped I understood his not answering.

 Business was slow at the Oasis. A total of three of us were drinking. And by the look of the lovebirds sitting at the end of the bar, the count would soon go down to one. I watched them kiss and swoon over each other and wondered if they were married. They both looked to be in their mid-ages. The man wore a suit and tie. The tie unknotted hung loosely around his collar. He had that stomach bulge that most men get in their middle age. The woman remained beautiful regardless of the wrinkles that settled in her skin. Her body was shapely, and her blond hair full and rich. They stared affectionately at each other. So, maybe they weren't married.

I sat sideways so I could get a good look inside the hotel's lobby. At eleven O'clock, Johnny Million walked in. He went straight for the elevator. I got up and watched the elevator stop on the second floor.

I approached the registration desk and thumbed the call bell on the counter. A man who looked older than the bartender peaked his head out the door of the room behind the desk. He looked at me with a dazed expression. Like a racehorse that ran the track going the wrong way.

"What can I do you for?" he asked.

"Hey, buddy, do me a favor. I got separated from a friend. We were riding the L-Train. Jesus, what a monster that thing is. Ever ride that train?"

The clerk nodded his head.

"Anyway, as I was saying, we got separated. I know his room is on the second floor, but try I as might I forgot the room number. Give me a helping hand and tell me the number, will ya? Johnny, his name is Johnny Million. Like one in a million." I laughed for effect.

The old man came wobbling out of the room. He took the registration book from a drawer and flipped open the pages.

"Room 235," he said without looking back up. I guess the strain of lifting his head was too much.

I went outside to my car for the policeman's sap I keep under the driver's seat. I put it in my hip pocket and walked back inside the hotel. A policeman's sap is a good weapon.

One hit across the jaw will stop the most aggressive troublemaker.

I took the stairs two at a time to the second floor and found Room 235 at the end of the hall. I put my ear to the door. When I heard the toilet flush, I kicked in the door. Johnny Million, his pants around his ankles, stumbled out of the bathroom. I hit him on the side of his head. I didn't mean to knock him out just damage his equilibrium. The man's legs went in opposite directions, and Johnny timbered like a giant sequoia tree to the floor.

I took hold of his shirt collar and lifted his head. "Who sent you to bump me off," I said.

His eyes glazed and rolled to the back of his head. I slapped him hard on the face.

"Don't you die," I screamed, and slapped him again.

Johnny Million's eyes never refocused.

He was dead.

I let his head down.

His dying didn't add up. Johnny Million was a big man-a strong man, and I didn't hit him hard enough to kill him. I looked him over. White foam bubbled from his mouth.

I went into the bathroom. Old hotel's like the Donnelly built before the addition of ventilating systems in bathrooms, installed windows to let out the obnoxious odors. The window was too small for a man to crawl through. A bottle of pills, which I took for aspirin, sat overturned on the sink. Two of the pills were different from the others — light pink and slightly smaller than the aspirin.

I stepped over the body and reached for the door, but a hard knock made by a hard fist stopped me from leaving.

"Open up, police," the harder sounding voice belonging to the hard fist demanded.

I pulled back my teeth and froze.

"Open up, or I'll break the door in."

To break in the door, he would have to use his shoulder or kick it in as movie cops do. But this wasn't a movie, and doors are strong. I knew he wasn't about to kick the door in because cops protected their feet more than any other parts of their bodies. Using his shoulder as a batting ram was also out of the question. His shoulder would crack long before the door would. I was betting that the cop would go down to the lobby and get a passkey. That would give me time. If the cop was working alone, I could sneak out of Million's room and disappear down the hall. I put my ear to the door. My bet wasn't pay off. I heard footsteps on the hallway running toward the door and then the sound of a key turning in the lock.

A detective, who I didn't know, walked in. He was tall, broad-shouldered, and burdened with a face, not even his mother would kiss. One eye closed halfway over with scar tissue and his nose flat and wide like he ran into a wall face first.

Another goon wearing a cheap costing brown suit accompanied him. The man was short with boyish looks and wavy blond hair.

"Going somewhere, Caruso?" the detective said.

"You know me, but I don't know you," I said smartly.

"Bradshaw," he said. "That one is detective Flagg."

"You know this mug rat, Lieutenant?" Flagg said.

"Caruso was a homicide cop," Bradshaw said, walking past me into the room. "Now he works at being a shamus. If you can call that work," Bradshaw said, kneeling next to Million.

"A private dick, huh?" Flagg put a hand on my chest and pushed me backward. "You weren't thinking of leaving a crime scene, were you Mr. private dick?"

"Do you know the stiff?" Bradshaw asked. He was busy feeling through the dead man's pockets.

"Johnny Million," I said. "He tried to kill me once upon a time."

"So, you returned the favor."

"I only wanted to have a friendly chat."

Bradshaw looked up over his shoulder at me. "Doesn't look friendly to me," he said.

"You two always wait outside hotel rooms?"

"We got an anonymous tip,"

"Anonymous sure gets around," I said.

Bradshaw looked at me sideways with his one good eye. "Frisk him, Osgood, and cuff him," he said. "You are under arrest for murder, Caruso. We'll hand deliver you to homicide."

"Osgood?" I said with a half sneer as detective Flagg ran his hands under my coat and down each leg. He lifted each pant legs to see if I was hiding an ankle holster. "You must get ribbed plenty carrying around a moniker like yours'."

That got me a punch to the gut and a second to the top of my head. The punches didn't stop until I stopped seeing them coming.

CHAPTER 32

Bradshaw and Osgood turned me over to homicide, and Shakespeare threw me in the hoosegow, bragging that he was going to throw away the key. I don't know what I ever did for him to dislike me as much as he does. But there I was sharing a cell with a drunk. According to the guard, my cellmate may or may not have killed his girlfriend.

Morning came, and with it came the medical examiner's report that Johnny Million died from poison, not a blow to the head. The pinkish pills I saw in the hotel bathroom were fast-acting poison. The knock to the head I gave Johnny only put him to sleep. He was walking dead when I clubbed him.

Shakespeare was not at all happy with having to set me free.

I wasn't happy being locked up.

It all evened out.

The squad room was relatively quiet for a sunny spring morning. The smell of tobacco and brewed coffee whiffed through the air. My stomach growled, reminding me that I hadn't eaten in twenty-four hours.

Shakespeare was sitting in his office, rubbing his toes and acting nonchalant for a man that only hours ago wanted to see me hung.

"What do you know about those two bums that brought me here last night?" I asked.

"Bradshaw and Flagg?" Shakespeare said. "They're a couple of gauchos from the 10th. Bradshaw has been around the block for a long time. Did you get a load of his face? He miscalculated a bust a few years back and got caught in a house fire. No one gave him much of a chance to pull out of it, but he did. The dude is too dam mean to die. Osgood Flagg is just a stooge."

"The stooge beat me up," I said.

Shakespeare shrugged.

"I think they tailed me to the hotel."

"That's your guess. Mine is I don't know."

"Them showing up seems suspicious," I said.

"Everyone is suspicious to you, Caruso. What I think is suspicious is the way Johnny Million died. Mugs the likes of Johnny Million go out in a blaze of bullets not by eating poison," he said. "Who kills someone with poison?"

"A woman," I said. "Poison isn't messy like shooting or stabbing. She doesn't have to be there to see him die."

"Bingo. Johnny Million must have a dozen dames that want to kill him."

"It only takes one," I said.

"What I don't understand is why Million ate the pills," Shakespeare said. "He must have seen the difference in color between the poison and aspirin. In his shoes, wouldn't you ask yourself, what gives?"

"Maybe not," I said. "How often do you look? You shake two pills out of the bottle and never look at what is in your hand. You swallow them down with a glass of water."

Shakespeare rolled his eyes. "Like a bad beat in poker, Million drew two pink pills instead of the white pills. If he were lucky and swallowed aspirin, you would have had a fight on your hands." Shakespeare slipped his shoe on. "There is one good thing to come of this," he said.

"And what is that?" I asked.

Shakespeare stretched his arms out wide and yawned. "You kill rats with poison, don't you? Now one less rat is running around the city."

"My guess is there is another rat," I said. "Cheesy Gorman."

"I never trusted Cheesy," Shakespeare said, scratching his nose. "His nickname fits the description."

"Cheesy, or someone he is connected to set me up."

"How do you figure?" Shakespeare asked.

"Cheesy called me out of the blue. He knew how deep I was in investigating Phyllis Steele's death, and he knew that Johnny Million tried to kill me."

"So, he sends you to the Donnelly Hotel to even the score with Million," Shakespeare said.

I nodded. "I took the bait. I go straight to the hotel wanting to take it to Million. To get him to confess on who paid him to shot me. But he's dead."

"Perfect timing," Shakespeare said. "Million swallows the poison. It acts fast and kills him just as you bust in his room. They wanted it to look like you killed Johnny Million,"

"And someone, maybe Cheesy himself, called Bradshaw."

"The anonymous tip," Shakespeare said.

Shakespeare leaned back in his chair. The wood creaked, resisting his weight.

"What you have, Caruso is a good old fashion ménage a trios. A hat trick. A threesome," he said. "Phyllis Steele, Johnny Million, and you. Well, almost you. I'm still holding out on that one."

"What do we do now?" I asked.

"Breakfast," Shakespeare said, sitting up, relieving the pressure on his chair. "I'm hungry, and when I'm hungry, I eat."

The city towed my car. The towing company, which locals have sarcastically named the Windy City Privates, wanted fifty bucks to get the Caddy out of hock. So I left it there. The car was out of gas anyway.

I rode with Shakespeare to the Howard Johnson restaurant at the Ohio House Motel on Ohio Street. Steam fogged the windows and the glass door of the restaurant. Stepping inside the breakfast smells of coffee and maple syrup was welcoming. Early morning customers were lined up at the counter, getting coffee and donuts to go.

The hostess sat us in a booth.

Shakespeare ordered eggs and bacon.

I ordered pancakes.

We both drank coffee.

"Breakfast is the most important meal of the day," Shakespeare said. "You should eat protein, not sweet pancakes."

"Why are you so interested in my nutrition?"

"Because on an empty stomach, you get grumpy. Pancakes initially fill your belly, but ware off as the day goes on. I don't want to have to listen to your belly growling."

Our orders came. Shakespeare worked on his plate of scrambled eggs and bacon. He pointed his fork at his food. "This is some good grub. How are those pancakes? You understand that kids eat pancakes, not adults."

I felt my stomach churn before I took my first bite.

I ate my pancakes, and I watched Shakespeare shovel the eggs and a triangle of toast into his mouth.

"So, what's next?" I asked.

Shakespeare wiped his mouth with a napkin. "Since when do you ask my advice?"

"That's why we're here. Isn't it?"

"I'm having breakfast. I thought you would like to join me."

"Are we going to see Cheesy, or what?"

Shakespeare pushed out of the booth. He wiped his mouth one last time and dropped the napkin down on his soiled plate.

"Sure. You're buying breakfast."

CHAPTER 33

We pulled to a stop in front of the Textile Outlet at noon on the button. Shakespeare squeezed out from behind the stirring wheel. Shielding his eyes with a cupped hand, he looked up to the sky. I followed him out of the car and started for the building entrance. The sun shone directly over our heads. Not a cloud in the sky, only the big blazing sun, and already the day sizzled.

"What a zoo," Shakespeare said.

Around us, 21st Street was a bustling caravan of people, trucks, and racks of men's suits, shirts, pants, and women's dresses in all colors and styles loaded into delivery trucks. One by one, the trucks pulled away from loading docks, their destination, department stores, and fashion boutiques in Chicago, and other cities throughout the states.

"Chicago is a major clothing manufacturer," I said. I reached the door and pulled it open.

"Never guess judging by the way you dress," Shakespeare said. There was a tinge of glee attached to his words. I let it fly by me.

A young woman, sitting at a desk, stood and approached us. She asked if she could help.

I refrained from using my regular snappy comeback. Shakespeare flashed his badge.

The girl examined it with a great deal of concentration. Her cheeks blushed, and her round eyes gleamed like she just discovered that the Tooth Fairy was real.

"Gosh, real detectives," she said.

"I'm the detective," Shakespeare announced and snapped shut his wallet. "He's a shamus."

The girl blinked. The expression on her fresh-face turned quizzical.

"I'm a private detective," I said, clearing up the meaning of shamus.

Her eyes grew round again. "Wow, like Sam Spade," she said.

"Yeah, like Sam Spade," I said. "We're here to talk to Cheesy."

Once again, her eyes flattened, and she looked confused.

"Mr. Gorman," I said.

"Oh, sure," she bubbled. "I'll take you to Mr. Gorman's office."

We followed her from the front of the warehouse to the back where the stairs went up to Gorman's office, and I couldn't think of better sights to see than her slender waist, tight hips, and stiletto legs in front of me. The girl looked about twenty-two years old. Her hair was wavy red in a modern style that fell across her big blue eyes. If her blouse came in a smaller size, her breasts would pop the buttons.

"I'm working in the warehouse until my modeling career takes off," Red explained. "Mr. Gorman is helping me break into the modeling business."

"I bet he is," I said

"Some nights, we work late, but I don't mind."

"I bet you do," I said.

Mr. Gorman is teaching me moves."

"Sure he is," Shakespeare said.

"Mr. Gorman is such a nice man."

"A real cream puff," we both said.

She wiggled her tosh, taking each step of the stairway as if the stairs were a fashion show runway. She stopped at the top of the stairs. "Mr. Gorman, two detectives here to see you," she announced. She pulled open the door and let out a high pitched scream. She let go to put her hands over her mouth, and the door shifted closed.

Shakespeare pushed her aside to bulldoze into the office. Red was crying when I brushed past her.

Cheese Gorman sat behind his desk as dead as anyone with a half a dozen Tootsie Roll suckers stuffed down his throat could be. His lips were blue, his face pale white, and his bloodshot eyes looked the way every strangled person's eyes look like after they breathe their last breath.

"Looks like Cheesy took third place in your trifecta, Shakespeare," I said.

He looked disappointed. "And I was counting on it being you," he said.

CHAPTER 34

Katrina and I lay in bed. The night turned chilly, so we pulled the blanket up to our chins.

"Does Shakespeare have a clue on who killed Cheesy?" she asked.

"Not an ounce of one," I said.

Katrina ran a finger down my chest.

"Have you forgotten about Julio Silva?"

"No I haven't. He gave me three days to get evidence that his sister didn't kill Domenic Conte. I've have one day left."

"And that day is tomorrow, and you're not worried," Katrina said.

"Julio may be tough, but he's no killer. At least that's my impression of the man."

"He might not be a killer, but he can punch hard," Katrina said, her voice sounded concerned.

"Yes, there is that," I said.

"Cheesy choked on Tootsie Roll suckers?" Katrina asked.

I held back a laugh, but a chuckle trickled out between my lips. Just the thought of Cheesy sucking on an all-day Tootsie Pop was a joke.

"Do you believe that?" I said. "He was trying to stop smoking. Sucking on Tootsie Pops took the place of smoking cigarettes. He joked that they would be the death of him. He was right about that. That wasn't much of a joke, after all."

Katrina sat up, letting the blanket slip down to her waist.

"Two people," she said.

I didn't hear. Katrina has a beautiful body, and I was too preoccupied with kissing her naked shoulder.

"Stop that and listen to me," she said.

I pulled her close and kissed her forehead. She wiggled away and pulled the blanket up to cover her.

"Do you want to hear what I think, or do you want to play?"

"If I listen now, can I play later?"

"Only if you don't fall asleep later," she said.

"I'll take those odds," I said. "I'm all ears."

"To push six lollypops down, a person's throat would take two people. One person does the pushing while the other person holds down the victim."

"What you're suggesting is that there are two people responsible for these deaths. Including Phyllis Steele and Johnny Million?"

"That's what I think," Katrina said, laying back down.

"You're right. Why didn't I think of that?"

Katrina took me by my arm and pulled me down to her.

"Two heads are better than one," she whispered.

"And what are you implying by saying that?" I asked.

She kissed my ear.

CHAPTER 35

In the morning, I shooed Katrina out of my apartment early. I didn't want her here when Julio Silva came around. I closed the door between the office, letting it swing open a crack. I went about fixing my office. The thick shade over the window behind my desk blocked sunlight from getting in, so I pulled it away to let some light inside. And then I sat down and waited. I put my forty-five revolver and a thirty-eight pistol on the desk in front of me both within quick reach.

An hour passed without Julio showing. Two hours passed and still no sign of the big man. I was about to call it quits when a man's shadow darkened the glass of the office door. I picked up the forty-five, and as the door opened, I leveled my gun chest high at Brooks Herrington.

"Don't shoot. Please don't shoot," pleaded Herrington stretching his hands above his head.

I came from behind the desk. "Get inside," I said, grabbing him by the arm and yanking him inside the office.

"No one followed me," he said.

"Call me skeptical for not believing you, Herrington," I said, poking my head into the hall looking both ways. The coast was clear, so I closed the door. "I've been looking for you."

Herrington lowered his hands "I went into hiding," he said. "You aren't the only one looking for me. I need a drink."

I nodded to the bottle on the desk. Herrington hustled to it and poured a hefty amount into a glass. He drained the glass of bourbon like it was ice tea.

"Okay, you've had your drink now fess up. What did you mean by saying I wasn't the only one looking for you?"

Herrington helped himself to a second pour. "There are those who want me dead."

Herrington sat down in one of the client chairs. On and off, he glanced at the door as if expecting someone to burst through it at any minute.

"Who's after you?" I asked.

"The same people that want me dead tried killing you."

"Who are they."

"They've killed before."

Herrington reached for the bottle, but I pulled it away.

"No more drink, Herrington, you've had enough. Your hands are trembling, your eyes are as wide as saucers, and your speech skips around like an irregular heartbeat."

Herrington swallowed hard like a man who was frightened about what lurked around every corner. I pinched a cigarette from the pack and placed it between Herrington's lips. I held a match to the end and watched the doctor suck on the filter until the other end glowed red. He released a long plume of smoke into the stale office air and watched the smoke as it floated over my head before he turned his eyes to the floor. I sat down next to him.

"Talk to me, Herrington. Who wants to kill you, and why?"

Doctor Herrington began talking. "As you know, I treated Phyllis Steele for two years. We tried various methods to cure her addiction. After each failure, I suggested hypnosis. Mrs. Steele agreed. During her first session, Phyllis spoke of a young woman named Maria."

"Maria Savona?" I asked.

"Phyllis didn't use her last name. Just Maria. When I questioned her about this woman, Phyllis confessed that her husband and his business partner unfavorably used this young woman."

"Did she name Jerry Pascoe outright?" I asked.

"No, but I assumed the man was Jerry Pascoe. Pascoe and Steele carried on a well-documented relationship. Who else would it have been?"

Herrington inhaled a nervous toke off the cigarette. "That was how the first session ended. Her second hypnosis session ended much the same-without drawing any conclusions or producing new answers. It was in the midst of her third session that Phyllis disclosed that Jerry Pascoe and her husband murdered a man in a hotel room."

The apartment door squeaked on old hinges as it budged a little wider. Herrington jumped off the chair. His face was as pale as a dead man's skin, and his eyes were bulging far out of their sockets. Herrington made ready to leap for the door when Lieutenant Shakespeare appeared in the apartment doorway.

"Did you hear all of that?" I asked him.

"Every word," Shakespeare said.

CHAPTER 36

Towering over the diminutive doctor, Shakespeare pushed Herrington back down into the chair and said: "I told you we would meet again."

Herrington, in a rare gust of spunk, struck back. "I told you then that I didn't kill Phyllis Steele, and I'm telling you that again now," he said.

Shakespeare, not one to back down from a fight, be it physical or verbal, trusted his hands in his pockets and circled like a cat playing with a defenseless mouse. "Maybe I can't nip you on murder charges, but I can on withholding evidence."

"But I'm telling you everything. Certainly, that counts for something, Lieutenant?"

"How do I know that what you're saying is true?"

"Phyllis Steele was under hypnosis."

"She could have faked it and made the whole story up," Shakespeare said.

"There is no faking hypnosis," the doctor said.

"How do I know what she said is even factual and not a hallucination?" Shakespeare questioned.

Herrington breathed deeply. His fatigue worn face shown scars of the verbal battle. His eyes revealed how taxing he felt running from those people who wanted him dead. And the torture that comes from drinking too much alcohol he wore like a mask. He opened his mouth to speak, and the words came out in one short, breathless sentence.

"Because she was in the hotel room when it happened."

Shakespeare stopped moving. His eyes wide in disbelief.

My breathing must have canceled because stillness fell over the room like a heavy blanket muffling all sounds.

Herrington smacked his dry lips bringing life back to our inanimate souls. "Can I get a drink?" he asked.

Shakespeare blinked and looked to me for confirmation. I nodded approval, and he handed off the bottle to the doctor.

With the appetite of a haji after days on the desert, Herrington swallowed a healthy mouthful of the booze. Quenched, he wiped his lips on his tailored shirt sleeve and politely handed the bottle back.

"What are you waiting for?" said Herrington shifting his eyes between Shakespeare and me. "Now, you have the evidence that you have wanted, so go and arrest Edward Steele."

I said: "You're very anxious about Steele's arrest. Is there more to the story that you haven't told us?"

Shakespeare made a fist out of his right hand and twisted it in the palm of his left, and his face twisted in an ugly snarl. "I'm listening," he said. Pulling over a chair, he sat in it and grabbed the bottle of bourbon off the desk, and took a swig.

Herrington crossed his arms over his chest. Suddenly, he was the conceited and overly confident prick I first met in Shakespeare's lockup. Suddenly, Brooks Herrington wasn't frightened. He was almost his arrogant self again. Was it my whiskey or his normal personality coming back to the surface?

Now I needed a drink. I reached for the bottle but stopped pouring. The truth fell me like a knockout from Julio Silva.

"And why should I tell you anything more?" Herrington said.

His eyes searched me like a pianist's fingers searched his keyboard for a lost note. But Harrington didn't have to say anything more. The expression of promise I held tight on my face told him that I knew what he wasn't telling us.

"You were blackmailing Phyllis Steele," I said.

"And how did you figure that out?" he asked.

I filled his glass and watched as he carefully lifted the glass to his mouth to sip.

"All criminals when cornered have a certain look," I said. "A particular thing they do with their body or a movement of their eyes that tattles on them."

"And I have those looks?"

"Yes, you have."

I lit a cigarette and passed the pack to Herrington.

"Yes, I did blackmail, Mrs. Steele," he admitted. His face stayed expressionless without a sliver of remorse showing in his eyes. And not one syllable did he utter in apology. He remained as thoughtless as a thief. "I took money and sex from her. Eventually, her cash on hand ran out, and I quickly became bored with lovemaking."

"So you killed her," Shakespeare said.

Herrington smirked. "Of course not. I would never look a gift horse in the mouth. I may have no longer wanted sex from Mrs. Steele, but I always wanted money. And Mr. Steele has lots and lots of money."

Shakespeare picked Herrington up off his seat and dragged the doctor to the door. "We'll throw you out and let the wolves have at you," Shakespeare said.

"But I don't know anything more," Herrington pleaded.

"Sure you do," I said. "Being under hypnosis is like taking a shot of truth serum. Phyllis Steele couldn't hold back spilling her guts and you helped her."

Doctor Herrington's face turned a shade of green I never saw before that moment. Shakespeare held Herrington so tight he cut off the doctor's wind. As soon as Shakespeare let him go Herrington dropped faster than a sack of flour landing on his knees. As he sucked air his fingers busied finding the top button on his shirt to loosen the collar.

I dragged over a chair and he sat in it. I drained what little remained of the whiskey into a glass and gave it to Herrington. The doctor caught his breath, drank and began telling us everything he knew. By the end of the day Shakespeare had enough evidence to arrest Edward Steele for the murder of Domenic Conte, Charge Terrance Johnson with conspiracy to cover up the murder, and put Herrington behind bars for blackmail. It was a good haul for the Lieutenant, but I wasn't any closer discovering who killed Phyllis Steele.

Shakespeare had Herrington on his feet clamping handcuffs on his wrists.

"Before the Lieutenant drags you off to jail, Herrington I want to know one thing. Did Julio Silva kill Phyllis Steele?"

Herrington's eyes fell on me like a closing gate. "No, he didn't kill Phyllis Steele," he said.

Shakespeare pulled him out of the room. I stepped out into the hallway to watch. Just before the elevator doors slid closed Herrington struck out a foot stopping the closure.

"Julio Silva didn't kill her," Herrington yelled back to me.

I ran down the hall and jumped inside the elevator just as the doors slid shut behind me. The elevator started moving downward.

"Because Phyllis Steele isn't dead."

The elevator stopped at the lobby floor and the doors whiffed open. Shakespeare pulled Herrington out to his waiting car.

"Where is Phyllis Steele?" I yelled.

Shakespeare pushed Herrington into the back seat.

"The Donnelly Hotel," I heard Herrington say.

Shakespeare turned back in my direction to say something, but I was out the back door and on my way to my car.

CHAPTER 37

I parked in front of the Donnelly Hotel, locking the car before going inside. The afternoon was warm with a cloudy sky that hazed over the sun like a thinly layered veil. No people were walking the sidewalks, or cars on the street. Birds didn't sing, nor did dogs bark. A couple of cats purred as they busied themselves nibbling on leftovers from an open tin of sardines. The only real sound came from an open third-floor window on the building across the street. A radio there perched on the ledge blared the play-by-play action of a pre-season baseball game.

I crossed the sidewalk to the door of the hotel. A sour smell blew my way from the garbage can the cats overturned. I pulled on the door and walked inside the hotel.

The musty odor of shopworn furniture mixed with the stink of cigarette smoke polluted the lobby air. I stuck my head inside the Oasis Lounge in the slightest chance Phyllis Steele might be there. One person sat at the bar. A man wearing a gabardine suit was drinking a bottle of beer. I turned back toward the reception desk and the old man that operated the counter. He saw me coming and sensed trouble. He was trying to duck behind the desk but I caught him on his way down. He looked up at me. His forced lie about stooping to pick up a dropped pencil didn't score with me. He stood up, resting his hands, palms down on the desk to steady legs that must have felt like Jell-O sticks.

There were five floors of rooms in the hotel. Phyllis Steele was in one. I described her to the desk clerk, but he shook his head. Swore on a stack of bibles that he didn't recognize the woman. I knew that he was lying to me, and he knew that I knew it. He tried squirming away, but I held him tight, pulling him over the counter. The welcome bell hanging over the entrance door tinkled as the door swung open. An elderly couple with suitcases in hand stepped inside. One look at me with my hands wrapped around the desk clerk's neck, and they walked back out.

The clerk didn't require much negotiation after that. He gave up room 318 as the room Phyllis Steele registered. However, Vanessa White was the name she used.

"You want the master key?" the clerk asked.

"Sure," I said. "And where is the desk phone?"

He pointed behind the counter. I grabbed the cord and pulled it out of the wall socket. I released the clerk, and he sat down on the floor. I went up to room 318.

I was about to use the master key to get inside the room when the door opened. Phyllis Steele stood in the open doorway. She looked surprised to see me. She also looked different. Blond hair replaced the brunette style. And her clothes were more casual than the clothes she usually wore. She dressed simply in a white blouse and dark colored slacks. The slacks showed her ankles and highlighted nicely with her shoes. The blouse showed other parts of her body equally as well. But not even the revised hairstyle or change of clothes could disguise her eyes. They were the same soft color of grey.

"I didn't count on seeing you when I opened the door," she said.

I said, "I didn't count on seeing you either. I heard you were dead."

I nudged her aside and walked into the room.

Johnny Million died in a similar looking room. The bathroom was in the same location as his room. This bed was a double and not a single like his, but the bedspread was the same color green. A chair was by the window the same place his was at. And an identical mirror hung over an identical four drawer dresser.

I pushed the door closed and went and sat on the bed.

"Take a load off," I said, patting the mattress beside me.

She didn't accept my invitation. Instead, she strolled across the room by-passing the bed and stopping at the dresser. On top were three bottles: one labeled gin, a second scotch, and the third bourbon. An ice bucket and four cocktail glasses sat beside them. Phyllis uncorked the bottle of bourbon.

"Can I buy you a drink?" she asked.

I wanted to keep a clear head, so I passed on the drink.

"Nonsense," she said. "I'm having one, and so are you."

She poured the drinks and then came as close to the bed as her arm could reach to hand me my glass. Turning, she went and sat in the chair by the window. She crossed her ankles and nursed the bourbon, letting her eyes size me up and down. They stopped on my mouth. I didn't know if she wanted to kiss or hit me.

"How did you do it?" I asked.

A wolfish grin that you would expect to see on the lips of a misbehaving child slipped across her lips. Knowing full well what I meant, she asked.

"Are you referring to my coming back to life?" And then she admitted. "That was easy. I have a twin sister."

"Vanessa White, is your sister?" I said.

Mine was not a wild guess, but putting two and two together. The registration clerk had told me the name.

"I thought you unpredictable, but killing your sister? That was a dreadful and evil-hearted deed."

"Don't misunderstand me, Joe, Vanessa may have been my sister by blood, but she was not my sister by spirit. We hated each other. Killing her was no big deal. But I didn't do it, of course. I left that chore to a professional."

"Like Johnny Million," I said.

She uncrossed her legs and planted both feet firmly on the floor.

"I wondered when you'd get around to him."

In the most straight forward way of putting it, I said. "You sent him to kill me."

"That was Edward's idea," she said. "You started snooping into his business."

"You are referring to Maria Savona and Domenic Conte?"

"You got too close, Joe. If only you played the game the way I intended the game be played, then sending Johnny wouldn't have been necessary."

"You killed him."

"Poor Johnny messed up. He wasn't the sharpest knife in the set, but I liked him."

"You like a lot of men. Do you use all the men that you like?"

"Not all," she said, standing. "You haven't tasted your drink," she said. "It's an excellent bourbon."

I blew up. Springing off the bed, I slammed the glass down on the nightstand, spilling the excellent bourbon to the floor.

"You used me," I barked. "You set me up, first with Julio Silva. You knew Silva would come looking for me. I was one of the detectives that put his sister in jail. He would be looking for revenge. All I had to do was wait for Silva to show. And when he did, you hoped I would kill him in self-defense.

Then there was that business with Brooks Herrington. Giving me his calling card with instructions to notify him to get in touch with you, what a joke that was. You waited for me to show up at Herrington's office, and when I did, you made your move. Katrina and I saw you there. We told that to Lieutenant Shakespeare. Our statement and your husband was all the identification needed to pronounce Phyllis Steele dead and cast an accusing finger at Brooks Herrington."

"Silva and Herrington. You would have gotten two birds with one stone and used me to do it to them except for one thing. Julio Silva hired me to find out who framed his sister for Domenic Conte's murder, and Brooks Herrington didn't get charged with murder. Herrington blew the whistle on you,

Phil. He's in jail, and the cops are on their way to arrest your husband and his lawyers."

Phyllis turned slowly to look out the window. She drank the last drops of bourbon in her glass and said.

"Edward got himself into deep financial trouble. He overextended himself and made bad investments. He owed more then he could pay. The people he owes money to aren't the type that repossess your mortgage. They take your life. He couldn't draw money from his business any longer, so I came up with this plan. Edward took out the insurance policy, and I invited my long lost twin sister to visit. We kill Vanessa, and I assume her identity. The insurance money would pay off our debt, and we still had money left over to disappear on."

She took a deep breath and let it out slowly. "You could let this go, Joe. Turn around and walk away, and you will become a rich man."

"I don't think I can do that," I said.

She turned from the window and stepped over to the other side of the room. Standing at the dresser with her back to me, she put her glass down next to the three bottles, the ice bucket, and the cocktail glasses. She slipped her hand into the top drawer and turned to face me. She pointed a gun at me.

"A dead man doesn't need as much money as a live man does. Is that it?" I said.

"Something like that," she said.

CHAPTER 38

She held the gun outstretched in front of her about shoulder high and aiming the thirty-eight at my chest. That was her first mistake. Any sudden movement from me would quickly knock the gun from her grasp before she could pull the trigger if she did manage to press off a round the bullet would miss its mark. I was about to make that move when I heard the door open. From my peripheral vision, I saw the blurred image of a man entering the room. Phyllis made her second mistake. She took her eyes off of me. For one brief second, she looked at the man in the doorway.

I dove to the floor.

A gunshot went off.

I watched as Phyllis Steele's expression changed from good looking and confident to surprised and pained. A red spot appeared on her white blouse above her left breast. The blotch quickly spread into a red stain.

Her gun was the first to drop to the floor. Phyllis followed next.

The ringing in my ears began to disappear along with the gun smoke. However, the pungent smell of gunpowder and the incense from spilled blood remained.

The smoking gun that fired the fatal shot belonged to Lieutenant Bradshaw.

"Whose side are you on, Bradshaw?"

"The side that pays the most," he said.

I reached for my holstered weapon.

Bradshaw warned, "No, don't do that. Stand up."

Bradshaw wore tight black gloves that fit his hands like a second skin. He stood close to me that I smelled the smoke coming from the barrel of his gun. He reached inside my jacket and removed my weapon from the shoulder holster.

I said, "So, it was you who killed those people, not Julio Silva."

Bradshaw pushed me up against the wall. His hands felt around my waist and over my legs for concealed weapons.

"Affirmative. You sure are smart."

"Did she pay you?" I asked, nodding at the dead woman on the floor.

"Why do you care?" he said.

"Professional courtesy," I said.

Bradshaw grunted. "Her and the husband," he said. "Turn around and face me."

"And now you're cleaning up the loose ends," I said.

"Something like that."

"Does that mean Edward Steele is dead?"

"Affirmative."

"Let me guess the way he died. Steele committed suicide. Am I right?"

"Affirmative."

"What about her?" I asked, referring to Phyllis Steele.

"You killed her with this gun," Bradshaw said.

"It will never stick," I said.

"It will stick all right. The desk clerk will vouch. He'll tell how you made a fuss in the lobby. You were looking for a woman. You threatened him in giving you a pass key to all of the rooms. You even ripped the phone line out of the wall so he couldn't call for help. But he used the phone in the lounge, and he called the police. The bartender and a man sitting at the bar saw everything, Caruso. I burst into the room and saw you shoot Phyllis Steele. We fought, and I knocked you out. I called homicide. The District Attorney can do the rest."

"It won't fly. I'll deny all of it."

"It will fly from here to the state prison and send you to the electric chair. You're as good as fried chicken, Caruso. Turn around. This will hurt."

CHAPTER 39

"You like doing things the hard way."

The words bumped around in my ears before my brain made two sense of them. I found myself on my back on the bed in the hotel room. A headache worked hard, keeping me from opening my eyes. My tongue felt swollen and dry. Blood soiled my fingers when I brought them away from my head. But I was alive.

"You like doing things the hard way," Shakespeare repeated. His voice had an ominous tone to it. Maybe I was worse off than I thought. I tried sitting up, but the abdominal muscles that controlled the movement reeked pain. Shakespeare pushed me back down.

"There isn't any hurry for you to get up," he said. He kept his hand planted on my chest. Insurance if I tried moving again.

Katrina's voice came loud from where I perceived the direction of the door. I tilted my head, resting my chin on my chest to see. She sat on the edge of the bed. Taking my hand, she kissed my fingers.

"He'll be okay," said a young doctor who arrived with the ambulance.

With the doctor's help, I managed to sit on the side of the bed. Next to the bed stood Shakespeare. Bradshaw sat in the chair by the window with his hands cuffed behind his back.

The coroner placed a sheet over Phyllis Steele.

"It worked," Katrina said. "You recorded every word that Phyllis admitted and Bradshaw said.

Shakespeare held the small tape recorder in his hand. The one Katrina gave me. I concealed the recorder in my pocket, turning it on when I walked into the room. I recorded every word Phyllis Steele said to me. The machine continued recording every word Bradshaw said.

"The higher up in the police force had their eyes on Bradshaw for a long time," Shakespeare said. He spits tobacco from his cigar. "He was dirty. Detective Flagg turned him in."

"Is Edward Steele dead?" I asked.

"Yes, he's dead," Shakespeare said. Bradshaw killed Edward Steele and the others, including Vanessa White, the twin sister of Phyllis Steele. He murdered her brutally. Beat her, so we believed that Julio Silva killed her."

"But, Bradshaw didn't kill Fredrick Ore," Katrina said. "Julio Silva killed him."

Katrina squeezed my hand, and I knew that Julio Silva was dead. I asked her how he died.

"Julio went to Pendleton's office intending to kill him," Katrina said. "He always considered that the three lawyers framed his sister. Julio wanted revenge. He would have killed you too, Joe. Amelia Pendleton was there in her brother's office when Julio burst through the door. Remember, she bragged to us about studying martial arts. Well, Amelia didn't lie. Somehow she overpowered the bigger man. She stabbed Julio in the heart with a letter opener from her brother's desk.

The good news, if there is anything good to be gotten from all of this, is Maria Savona will soon get out of jail."

Shakespeare said: "I talked with the District Attorney. He wants to hear the tape recording, but there isn't any doubt that Maria Savona will be a free woman within the next 24 hours."

"Just in time to bury her brother," I said.

"You did good work, Caruso," Shakespeare said. "But next time, try not to get your light's punched out."

He glanced over to the covered body of Phyllis Steele.

"I heard she was dead."

"So did I," I said. "So did I."

THE END